A TASTE OF MAGIC

MAGIC OF THE DAMNED

MCKENZIE HUNTER

This is a work of fiction. Names, characters, businesses, places, events, and incidents are either the products of the author's imagination or used in a fictitious manner. Any resemblance to actual persons, living or dead, or actual events is purely coincidental.

McKenzie Hunter

A Taste of Magic

© 2023, McKenzie Hunter

McKenzieHunter@McKenzieHunter.com

ALL RIGHTS RESERVED. This book contains material protected under International and Federal Copyright Laws and Treaties. Any unauthorized reprint or use of this material is prohibited. No part of this book may be reproduced or transmitted in any form or by any means, electronic or mechanical, including photocopying, recording, or by any information storage and retrieval system without express written permission from the author/publisher.

Cover Artist: Orina Kafe

For notifications about new releases, *exclusive* contests and giveaways, and cover reveals, please sign up for my mailing list at mckenziehunter.com

ISBN: 978-1-946457-46-2

ACKNOWLEDGMENTS

"Books are a uniquely portable magic."
—Stephen King, *On Writing: A Memoir of the Craft*

I would also like to extend my appreciation to my readers for continuing Luna and Dominic's journey. I am eternally thankful to my amazing beta readers: Elizabeth Bracker, Marcia Silva, Robyn Mather, Toni Glitz, Sherrie Simpson Clark, and Stacey Mann, who generously dedicate their time to assist me with my stories. I am also extremely grateful to my editors and proofreaders for their invaluable help with my books.

1

The casual room we sat in was a clear abandonment of Ileana's usual style. Walls a creamy shade of ivory, cozy cloudlike sofa and chairs, calming artwork adorning the walls, and taupe-color velvet curtains added warmth to the room and made a peaceful setting. What I felt, though, was diametric to the calm the room attempted to create. Ileana's long manicured nails drumming on the arm of her chair became the soundtrack for the tense silence that surrounded us.

Dominic and I sat on a sofa across from her as she sank back into the club chair. Dominic's brows furrowed together while he studied his mother intently. Time ticked by; he and I seemed to share the same unease of not knowing what was going through her mind.

I was saddled with the feeling that my life was seconds away from another upheaval. Things were bad. We had planned to siphon Peter's magic, but instead the Dark Caster stole both his magic and mine. The supernaturals were vying for a war. Dominic's father and sister had aligned with Peter, in the expectation of getting power from him. Shades were now roaming the city with the ability to take on a human body, disguising themselves while keeping their immense magic. War was still looming between those on the side of the Conventicle and those with the New Conventicle. Dominic and I had retreated to the Vita, a section of a world that existed parallel to mine. I wondered if in the hours of our absence humans had discovered the existence of supernaturals.

Dominic's lips lifted into a humorless smirk. "This is complicated," he said, his voice a low growl. It was more than a simple complication. The situation incited anger in him that was threaded through his words. The fiery blaze in his eyes smothered when he closed his eyes. When he opened them, they were piercing and predatory. Did he have a plan or was that just a thirst for retribution?

Studying his contemplative frown, Ileana's somber expression darkened. Her eyes narrowed and the deleterious energy couldn't be ignored. "Do you want me to take care of this, Dominic?" her gentle tone finally asked. Her calming, sweet voice belied the menace that dwelled in her eyes. Her help would come in the form of unbridled violence and the loss of many lives. Except for Helena and Dominic, no one would be safe. She would take joy in adding Areleus, who I was now convinced she barely liked, to the people who'd fall victim to her help.

Several minutes passed while Dominic studied his mother, whose expression offered nothing more than a placid landscape. He shook his head.

"No, I will handle it, but I may need your help."

Some of my worry lifted knowing Dominic would be navigating this turbulent situation, not the woman with a penchant for survival of the fittest methods where she believed in the most destruction and had little regard for the lives that would be lost. She never considered changing her strategy even after I pointed out that humans were at a disadvantage. I wasn't naïve to Dominic's dark side, either.

He was the product of Ileana and his father and just as capable of being cold, calculated, and violent with ease. The difference was that he seemed to be the most reasonable of them all, and I trusted him.

"Of course, Areleus and Helena need to be involved as well," Ileana asserted in a tone that left no room for debate.

Dominic's jaw clenched. He and his father were at war, and the mention of his name made me relive the overwhelming fear I felt when Areleus had secured me against his chest, one hand around my throat and his claws at my stomach, to force Dominic's hand after he'd restricted Helena's magic. Once Helena's magic had been returned, she did everything possible to make Dominic regret giving her access to it again. How could he ally himself with his father and his sister, when they'd tried to kill him? I detested Helena. Her allegiance had proven to be the most variable and insidious. She aligned herself with whomever she determined would be the victor. Helena's loyalty wasn't to a person but to their potential for success.

"No." Dominic matched Ileana's uncompromising tone.

"Son, that wasn't a suggestion. You must put aside your differences or you will fail. Kill your father after you've succeeded." She gave him a pointed look. "Helena must be spared. Understand, she will be loyal to you once you are in power."

"Or at least until someone else comes along who she suspects might have more power. Then the betrayal starts all over. An infinite loop," I mumbled, earning a sharp glacial look from her.

"Did you have something to say, Luna?"

Feeling overly protective of Dominic to a flaw, I repeated myself.

Her pointed look eased into a bemused half smile. "My magicless little creation is human once again."

Damn, the disdain she had for people who didn't possess a sliver of magic was tragic.

"You still remain quite bold even when you have no means of protecting yourself." The smile warped into a cruel chastising sneer.

I could say whatever disparaging thing I liked about Areleus, but she drew the line at Helena. Somehow, Ileana found some virtue in Helena choosing to side with power. Clearly, we valued different things.

"How can Dominic trust them? You're requesting he handle this volatile and dangerous situation while also dealing with the person who stole Dark Caster magic, and while having to watch my back at all times."

"Dominic won't have that worry because he'll have my protection—"

"Unless it involves Helena. She seems to get a pass on all her wrongdoings."

Despite being nearly feral in my protectiveness, I quickly realized it was a stupid and precarious place to be. My life had been put in peril on too many occasions. I wanted to decrease the chances of it happening again. But I couldn't rein in my turbulent emotions or my scathing opinions. Trusting Helena and Areleus would inevitably lead to more betrayal, violence, instability among humans and supernaturals, and my life being in danger. Ileana was growing impatient with my insolence, and the look she levied in my direction warned me to proceed with caution.

"Helena will obey my demands," Ileana asserted.

"Is there another side of her I have not yet met? Because the one I know doesn't seem to listen to anyone."

Ileana's cool look of displeasure turned from me to Dominic as if she was urging him to intervene.

"Luna is right. Helena is not to be trusted, and I won't give her another opportunity to betray me again. If you want her life spared, don't put her in a position to betray me. If it happens again, I won't show her any mercy."

"I can assure you that she won't."

Where was this confidence coming from? None of my dealings with Helena gave me any confidence that she would uphold her mother's request. But Ileana's assertion was made with the reverence of promise. I was curious as to how she'd achieve that oath, but I doubted she'd share. Perhaps she had a mom-request she could use that demanded compliance at all costs. Who knew?

"Will they make it a priority to protect and preserve humans?" Since they had so little respect for humans, I had to continue to be an advocate.

"Humans are not involved in this," she countered.

"Yes, they are. Hiding the existence of magical beings seems to be top priority, but with everything that's happened, I'm not sure that can continue. What happens to humans when it fails? Can their safety be guaranteed?"

The factions were split between the Awakeners who wanted to be revealed and place humans in a subservient role, and the Conventicle and New Conventicle and their acolytes, who were separate factions with the same goals. They wanted to continue anonymity for different reasons and approached the goal with extreme tactics.

"Luna's family must be protected." Dominic's response was achingly cool with the need to protect the people dear to me. He may not have shared his mother's dismal view of humans, but preservation of their lives had never been a priority.

"Not just my family. Humans cannot be casualties of this. It's not fair," I entreated, looking to Dominic for understanding.

"I don't seek to kill off humans," Ileana provided before he could respond. It was a far cry from what I wanted, which was a commitment to do whatever was necessary to save them. I gathered from her expression that was the best offer she'd give, which she punctuated with a dismissive shrug before leaving the room.

Dominic's fingers linked mine in a firm hold, deterring me from going after her and demanding more. It had been a fleeting thought, but I had no intention of pursuing it.

2

After our exchange with Ileana, I managed to force down the meal prepared for me, because I needed to eat despite my anxiety making food the last thing on my mind. Dominic picked at the food in front of him, cementing my hypothesis that they didn't need to eat but chose to.

Once we—rather, I—had eaten, we retreated to the bedroom where we showered and lay naked side by side, peering up at the ceiling.

"I need this to end. It's a bother," he said, exasperated, his forearm draped over his forehead. His comment was expressed with the glibness of someone receiving a burger with mustard when he requested it without—a nuisance but not a life-threatening situation.

"It's more than a *bother*. It's a dreadful situation. One that a lot of people, humans and supes, aren't likely to survive." Turning onto my side, I inhaled the hint of eucalyptus from the soap that lingered on his skin and wafted in the air. Small droplets of water glistened in the grooves of his abs and chest. His towel-dried hair was in disarray. The enormous bed looked diminutive with Dominic's massive muscular frame in the middle of it. He and his body were a sinful distraction I didn't need. He removed his arm from his forehead and turned to face me, his eyes intense.

"You survived." His voice was more teasing than I'd expected. A small smile curled at his lips.

"That's not surprising to you?"

He shook his head. "You've proven to be more resilient than you look." I frowned at his compli-sult. *I see what you did, prince.*

His rumble of laughter drew my eyes to where they always seemed to drift when he was naked: to the intricate patterns of ink that covered his body. Smiling at the effort it took for me not to trace them with my finger, he pulled me closer. His hardness pressed into me. His voice low and inviting as he growled my name. Entranced by his dark and unyielding amber eyes, I stayed locked with them.

We hadn't had alone time together since entering his mother's realm. I felt the absence of him. I shoved down the unease it raised.

"I'm glad you did," he said. "I must keep it that way."

"You have a plan to do that?" I had no doubts that he did. He'd said it with the same assurance Ileana had regarding Helena's loyalty. I had confidence in his plan, and none in Ileana's because hers hinged on a mercurial Helena.

"I have many, but one involves shared mutual destruction."

"As in a nuclear option? Never a good idea. How is that any different than any of Ileana's strategies?"

Shuddering with pleasure at his fingers roving over my body, leaving a trail of warmth with every touch, I was still determined not to let him distract me.

His lips pressed against mine. Soft, a gentle comforting touch that quickly became ravenous and hungry as his tongue explored mine. Seeking more, he pressed harder into me. I pulled away, panting, insistent in my goal to find out the specifics.

He smirked at my not so-hidden withering willpower. *Why is he so sexy and distracting?*

"My mother won't be as brazen in her destruction as you've been led to believe. And it's because she likes you and holds value in what is important to you." Once again, this family was using words wrong. Dictionaries for everyone for Christmas.

"*Likes*—or *tolerates* me enough not to kill me? Or does she love you enough not to be wholly destructive because of your feelings for me?" I asked.

"I'm very aware of my family's shortcomings. My affections for you would not have much bearing on how she'd deal with you or value your beliefs if she didn't like you. Her fondness just looks different than what you're used to. Your kind tends to display emotions in a strange manner."

I'm the strange one here.

Getting a pass on being murdered by Ileana was like a gentle hug and kiss from her. Our conversation was a reminder of how vastly different my life had looked a month ago. I missed that life of blissful ignorance and relative safety.

"If it's shared mutual destruction, how is that any different than your mother's suggestions?" I probed, my concentration dissolving in a quicksand of lust as his thumb stroked over my nipple. *Focus.* Heat coursed through me, making me wet between my legs. His hand languidly traveled in that direction before I took hold of the distracting appendage, ignoring the desire to give in and feel his fingers caress and stroke me there.

Stay on topic. Focus.

"Answer my question," I insisted, my voice a low rasp as I pushed logic to win out over a primal need that wanted to be satisfied. That *needed* to be satisfied.

"Because it's my last resort, not my first."

"What is your first resort?"

"Tomorrow. Let's discuss it tomorrow because nothing

can be done about it now." He kissed me in a way that managed to be both aggressive and soft. It seemed as if we had the same desire to extinguish the remnants of the tumultuous day. Sinking my fingers into his hair, I pulled him closer. Rolling me to my back, he pulled away, his gaze devouring every inch of me.

My nipples responded to his salacious attention. Hunger in his eyes, he cupped my breasts, his tongue teasing my hardened peaks. Intoxicating heat slid over them. They throbbed with pleasure. I quivered at the gentle nips and the cloak of magic that accompanied his touch. His hands moved lower, dragging a low moan out of me. Dominic's fingers were liquid warmth as he stroked me, a smile curling his lips as I gasped, grinding into his erotic touch, seeking more pleasure. Needing his skilled fingers to bring me satisfaction. He brought me to the edge before sliding down my body, planting wet kisses on me before spreading me open and nestling his face between my legs. Dominic's sensual flicks of his tongue over my engorged nub pushed me closer to the precipice of pleasure. Tantalizing kisses and fervent licks of his tongue coursed blissful heat through me until I succumbed to a climax.

He rose to his knees, positioning his hips between my legs. A satisfied groan escaped as I quickly accommodated his long length and thickness before we found a perfect synchronized rhythm, his fingers digging into my skin. Fire of desire danced in his amber eyes, his thrusts becoming more frenetic as he pushed deeper, seeking more pleasure.

Shivers of ecstasy ran along my spine. I panted and let out a surprised noise when he covered my body, rolling onto his back and taking me with him. Positioned into a straddle, I felt the full length of his hard cock. Dominic's hands palmed my breasts, stroking and teasing before gliding slowly down my body and settling on my hips as we hit an erotic rhythm of my movements. Each stroke more intense and pleasing.

"Fuck," he growled, his smoldering gaze searing into me. My senses were heightened, each movement, touch, stroke, and curl of his fingers into my skin igniting my need. Seeking a climax, our movement became unbridled heat and frenzy.

My body shuddered with the first pulse of my climax which lingered into a loop of pleasure that Dominic felt as I contracted on him. The final orgasm rocked me, and I found a peculiar exhilaration watching the Prince of the Underworld quake with intensity.

His satisfied body was languid and relaxed, a contrast to his heavy breathing. I slumped on the sheets, exhausted in my orgasmic haze. He nibbled at my shoulder and caressed me. Tender hands snaked over my body. Dominic's look was hungry, promising more encounters to come. Along with my intense pleasure was the heightened awareness that there was no denying or walking away from, because I had fallen completely for him.

3

———

The next morning, we revisited the activities of the previous night and managed to get a shower in as well. The sex was a form of escapism, but with each intimate coupling…there was more. I could see it in the way he looked at me; between the passionate, intense sex were furtive glances and soft caresses. And the words he held back, replacing them with touches and strokes that conveyed his emotions.

Dominic was insatiable, so I was tasked with pulling him from his languid exploration of my body as I attempted to get dressed. Through the distractions we managed eventually to get clothed. Turning to face him, I laced my fingers through his.

"What's the alternative to the mutual destruction?" My curiosity was alive and ready to be sated.

"Peter," he breathed out in a reluctant sigh. The apprehension was heavy in his words. "I need to determine how his magic was stolen without using a Garon, which only works when it's in contact with the person you're taking magic from. Magic was taken from you both without the Garon or touch. I suspect he may know the answer."

A shiver ran through me as I relived the strong, portentous magic that had overtaken mine, binding me to Peter and ripping it away from us both.

"Do you think he knew of the other Dark Caster?" I asked.

"You'd have a better idea than I would." His penetrating gaze held mine, searching my face, before his brow lifted in inquiry.

I considered my interaction with Peter prior to me attempting to divest him of his magic. I shook my head. "If he knew he hid it well. He seemed to genuinely want a partner in this."

Dominic frowned. "I don't think it was romantic. His only attraction was to the power and getting control over the supernaturals."

Annoyed, I exhaled. I was becoming increasingly irritated recounting Peter's impassioned soliloquies. My mind had been playing them in a loop since his name was mentioned. "Years of him blathering on about history being written by the victors, the ruthlessness of mankind, and accosting people with his unfiltered and unrequested lectures on history, only to be just as cruel and ruthless."

Dominic smirked at my rant. "That's with humans. Perhaps he holds humans to a different moral standard. The rules and expectations aren't the same because we have similar gifts."

"Not really. Your gifts exceed most. And I don't think you prey on people." I was being a little liberal with the use of *prey*. Dominic didn't prey on others, but he had no problem demonstrating his power and using it for coercion. Although he also kept his word and attempted some forms of fairness.

He nodded, although I wasn't sure he believed that to be true. "I'm not my father." If he found solace in that, good.

"He's ruthless." I said the part that was left unspoken. Dominic's expression hardened and he put a lot of effort in softening his furrowed brow and clenched jaw. The hold he had on my hand was increasingly tight and uncomfortable.

"Ow," I whispered.

"Sorry."

"It's fine."

The tacit conversation between us expressed more than we'd said in that exchange. To dethrone his father, Dominic would have to become just as ruthless. And I'd see a side of him that I hadn't yet seen. I'd said it was fine. But would it be?

Patricide. When I thought of fathers, a warmth swelled in me. My dad's quirky ways, his overt affection for my mother, and his tight, comforting hugs. That was what fathers meant to me. Dominic didn't have that kind of relationship with his father. He wouldn't be killing a person like my dad, but a father who had betrayed him, used me as a pawn to hurt him, and brutally attacked him. Their relationship was anything but typical.

With a tight smile, Dominic guided me out of the room, his fingers twined with mine as we walked to the dining area. Once in our seats, we were given plates with French toast, bacon, and an assortment of berries. My stomach growled at the sight of the food, but I couldn't pull my attention from the woman who served it. Her pale coral skin was complemented by russet-color low-coifed hair. Vivid, wide brown eyes and vulpine features were distinctive but human-like, if I ignored the fluttering butterfly wings. I thought they were just ornamental until she used them to retreat to the kitchen.

Sabin, who was sitting across from us, offered a wry smile before picking up his nearly untouched plate and leaving. His departure felt like he was fleeing rather than deciding to have his meal elsewhere. With Sabin gone, my attention moved to the lavish dining area and kitchen that reminded me of Dominic's focus on Ileana's created and their unsuccessful attempt to be unobtrusive.

This place is creepy. I wanted desperately to be more fascinated and intrigued by the created but couldn't manage to get past them unsettling me. Despite my introduction to shifters, witches, vampires—even a soiree with shades, the weirdest of the weird—I still found her creatures simultaneously beautiful and discomfiting.

Shoving a forkful of French toast into my mouth, I had the indulgent tastes of butter with hints of vanilla and cinnamon turn to sawdust at the sight of Areleus and Helena entering the room. I gulped water, forcing the mouthful down. Dominic stopped mid-bite, his eyes searing over his father and giving little regard to his sister who greeted him with a warm, insouciant smile devoid of any traces of remorse for her betrayal. She turned the same smile to me, and I responded with a glare. If he couldn't hate his sister, I was more than willing to hate her doubly on his behalf.

Dominic managed to school his murderous scowl into a cool look of indifference that mirrored his mother's, who had glided in next to her daughter. The similarities in their appearance were so stark that Ileana had to see herself in Helena every time she looked at her. Maybe that explained her insistence on leniency for Helena's behavior.

"I intervened since I wasn't confident that you'd call on your father and sister for assistance."

"You were right." Steeled hostility filled Dominic's words. He pushed his nearly full plate aside. Well, he might not need food to function, but I did. I scarfed the remainder of my breakfast despite the rising feeling that in minutes I'd be in the middle of unfettered violence between Dominic and Areleus. Dominic's claws emerged in protection. It took several beats of slow breathing before they receded.

"We need to figure out how to recapture the shades so they can't be used by the person who now possesses Luna's and Peter's magic," Areleus stated, approaching the table with an aloof confidence that wasn't warranted by the situation.

Read the room, man.

He'd known his son longer than I had, so how could he miss the calculations in Dominic's expression? There was nothing reassuring about Dominic's calm, which was just the peace before a blistering storm that encouraged approaching without fear. Areleus was ruthless, cruel, and had years of knowledge including the skills of self-preservation, yet he wasn't exhibiting any of those attributes today.

"Has there been any activity?" Dominic managed in a tight voice.

"The New Conventicle and the Conventicle appear to have unified. A common enemy seems to do that," Helena offered.

Dominic offered a cool assessing gaze in response before a cynical smile lifted his lips. "It's good to know that people ally for a common goal and not because they are power hungry. That I can understand and respect."

Helena swallowed her retort and pressed her lips into a rigid line.

It was a fragile union between the Conventicle and New Conventicle, which was hungering for power and just waiting in the wings. Could people who wanted to seize your position of authority be trusted?

Ileana's speculative gaze traveled over the royals' faces, the hostility-filled room deepening her frown. *What exactly did she expect?* Areleus and Dominic had every intention of determining who would be the official ruler of the Underworld under any violent conditions necessary. Helena would ally with the victor, whoever it was, although I suspected she preferred Areleus who would continue to allow her cruel behavior with impunity. Although Ileana clearly had no more use for Areleus, he'd help her create weapons that could ward off any invasions.

"I doubt we can do anything with that fractured alliance," Dominic said.

His father smiled and nodded, stepping forward to extend his hand to Dominic. Jerking his eyes to the proffered olive branch, Dominic stared, then dismissed it by turning an expectant look on his mother.

"Tenuous alliances are difficult to manage, which is why I made sure it was inevitable by releasing the prisoners from the Perils. If that doesn't work, I'll release the ones they were tasked with imprisoning," Areleus provided before Ileana could offer any explanation for her interference.

Dominic narrowed a hard gaze on his father. An assassin's final look through the scope. *I had the sneaking suspicion Ileana was the instigator of Areleus's decision to release the prisoners, because she kept a keen eye on the two of them like she was expecting the hostility to escalate quickly.*

Before Areleus could defend his actions, Ileana spoke up. "The Conventicle, along with their counterparts, will have to work together if they don't want to fall victim to the released prisoners' vengeance. Their focus on staying alive will strengthen their alliance more than their shared dislike for the Dark Caster, which at this time is an unknown. It's difficult to forge a bond over an unknown. They need to understand the threat. Some of them have been victims of Vadim's, Roman's, and Celeste's cruelty and recklessness, or know victims of, so they will be motivated to prevent more losses." Her lips quirked into a knowing smile. "*And*, this person with immeasurable powers isn't going to go after lowly witches, shifters, and vampires. The others—" She rolled her eyes. "The Awakeners, petulant children who don't see the value of anonymity, are not the majority or the strongest from what I understand. Forcing them to join the alliance. The three sects will be unified. Once this situation is over, keep it that way. It is beneath us to be so involved in their matters. Discover other ways to entertain yourself."

"I thought you weren't going to be involved," Dominic said.

"I'm not. I simply provided a strategy and set things in motion for the best outcome. It is a better approach than"—she looked at me, her smirk more pronounced—"descending into chaos and murder or setting off a magical carpet bomb. I've made things decidedly better," she said, paraphrasing the accusations I'd made about her previous strategies.

But did you?

Only having had a fleeting moment of magic, I felt like an island whose sole purpose now was to be the voice of humanity, because these people had proven that in situations like this, they were too far removed from it to care about those they deemed the lowest of them all. Humans.

Somehow, I'd failed and had to reluctantly accept that things would devolve into cruelty and unbridled violence. It was now about harm reduction. Now, I felt compelled to be the voice of reason and arbiter for minimal violence.

"Roman's claws still affect us," Dominic pointed out. "How will that make things better when I have to deal with his retaliation? I'm the one he hates the most."

Helena smiled. "It's handled. He isn't the threat to us that he once was. I couldn't undo that tricky witch's spell, but I performed an unbinding spell that I believe will disrupt the spell enough for it not to have the same effect." She gave an appreciative nod in her mother's direction, who I assumed had given her the means to do so. Ileana giving Helena more magical arsenals to cause trouble wasn't in the 'decidedly better category.'

"Did you test it?" Dominic challenged with a sneer. Roman's poisonous claws rendered the royals magicless until it wore off.

Helena lifted her chin in defiance. "I'm confident in my skill. But I suggest staying away from them as a matter of practice."

Her advice just revived images of her stabbing her

brother with her own claws. Based on the piercing look he gave her, it did the same for him as well.

Ileana waved a hand. "With the prisoners at large, I believe you will have the willing support of all three sects. As a unit, you will be dealing with exceptional power and skills, which will be a deadly challenge. If you three can't manage to squash any mutinous intentions and subdue them, do you deserve to live?"

Harsh.

"The shades?" Helena looked at her mother expectantly as if she was now at the helm of this situation.

"They should never have been allowed to exist. If I'm not mistaken, they were drawn to our little harbinger of that particular magic." As expected, all eyes turned to me. "And that very magic allowed them to escape. Whatever plans one might have for harnessing the shades for use needs to be abandoned. They are a liability. Destroy them," Ileana proposed. "Considering all that has occurred, I don't think it's just about the humans' supernaturals but us as well. Our magic is strongly linked to this world. If it is destroyed, it will affect our magic and our standing. The Dark Casters should have all been destroyed. They are the only ones who truly challenge us in a concerning way. Our concern shouldn't have been with the humans' supernaturals. Let the humans handle their messes. They will never have any bearing on us. The Casters are our problem. I'm sure the acquisition of Peter's and Luna's magic is in preparation to destroy us and our residency."

Letting the words settle in, Ileana shook her head in disbelief at the possibility. She looked at Dominic. "I stand by my initial plan. Let the Dark Casters make their ruin for thirty days, maybe sixty, when they will have sated their need for destruction and limited their pool of potential allies. They can't help themselves. But apparently, that is too inhumane." I earned another look from her. My feelings toward her were complex. I admired her directness and unwavering decisiveness but was appalled by her apathy about others. It was a strong fifty/fifty split. Part of me believed her suggestion earlier was for shock value, to prod Dominic into extreme action to preserve the integrity of the world we knew—they knew.

"You're not going to help?" Areleus asked.

She shook her head.

"If the Dark Caster manages to get here, do you have any plan for self-preservation?" Areleus asked.

She considered his question. "I won't leave mine. If I'm confronted, it is a sign that you three have failed. It is likely that I won't stand a chance. But my demise won't be as a result of me protecting people I don't particularly care about."

That fifty/fifty split was now at a firm thirty/seventy. I definitely felt more appalled than admiring.

She headed for the exit but stopped, looking over her shoulder at Dominic. "Remove the ward you placed at the entrance." He'd placed a second layer of protection that served as a warning to deter the uninvited from entering, or at least to rethink their decision, knowing that if they entered they might not leave.

Defiance blazed and then withered in his expression before he nodded. He had more pressing fights ahead of him.

With that, she departed, not allowing for further debate or questions. I didn't know if she'd 'set things in motion,' but she had done something. Whether it was good remained to be seen.

4

Ileana's exit appeared to be an invitation for the suppressed hostility to explode.

Areleus cocked an expectant brow at Dominic and extended his hand to him again.

Dominic locked eyes with him as he stood. "We will work together because it is advantageous. Your handshakes are as valueless as your words." He removed the smidge of space that remained between them. "If you ever touch Luna again you will no longer have any value to me, no matter the situation. I will kill you." Dominic was quickly at my side, taking my hand in his. I hopped to my feet, sidling in next to him as he breezed past his father and made a stop in front of his sister. "The same goes for you."

Her mouth opened and closed several times, puffing out huffs of breath in a poor attempt to control her anger and astonishment. Before we could get out of her presence, she'd stepped in our path. Astonished, turbulent wide eyes fixed on me and then jerked to Dominic. She might have been rendered speechless for a moment, but she gathered her words and they fell freely.

"You've chosen her over me?" she hissed out in disbelief.

"Who stabbed me? Who joined Peter? You're here now because that didn't work to your advantage, not because of regret. My statement stands. Touch her and I will kill you."

"I stood with the person who will bring about change. Who'd allow me to be more than a babysitter."

Dominic smirked, shook his head, and navigated around his sister. Seeing that his brisk steps had me nearly jogging to keep up, he slowed them to match mine. Used to the difference in our stride length, I'd adjusted by walking faster. His thumb made delicate strokes over my skin.

"Babysitters. That's what we've been reduced to!" she shouted after him.

Unmoved by her outburst, he continued to the bedroom we'd slept in. Once we were in the room, he devoured the small space between us, walking me back until my back pressed against the wall. His hand placed above my head as he leaned into me.

His head dropped and the tension became unbearable. He lifted his head, drawing his eyes up to meet mine.

"Luna." There was a tone of entreaty in his voice. He took a long, measured breath. "Be prepared for things not to go as you'd wish. Not everyone can or will be saved. I can't accommodate your human sensibilities." Were they attributes that only humans felt? Causing the least amount of harm seemed like a basic tenet of existence. Apparently, I was wrong. After a long pause, he added, "I doubt they'll go as I'd hope, as well."

Hearing the resignation in his voice, I knew he was preparing me for the worst, but I had no idea what that looked like. I was sure humans would be affected and undoubtedly a number of supernaturals as well.

This was a mess caused by one person.

Helena's and Areleus's expressions were placid while Dominic instructed them to deal with the Conventicle, New Conventicle, and Awakeners and to assure formation of the alliance.

"If the Awakeners don't readily comply they will need to be dealt with swiftly and efficiently," Areleus said. His words cemented my growing apprehension about him and Helena being involved in any of it.

Dominic's flat expression remained. He'd conceded to the reality that Areleus had lost any semblance of civility and that every decision Areleus made was about the acquisition of power and diminishing the strength and abilities of anyone who would oppose him, including Dominic.

"What will you be doing during our tedious work?" Helena asked.

Not fully trusting his father and sister with information, he gave a tepid smile. "I'm going to find a secure place for Luna, deal with the shades, and handle the Dark Caster."

Areleus sneered. "An ambitious goal. Why do I suspect you have plans that you're not sharing with us?" A slow grin quirked his lips. "Will the Book of Umbra be used?" A covetous expression cast a dark look over his face. Dominic was the person standing between him acquiring a book with dangerous spells and even worse consequences for the invoker of the spells.

Dominic's eyes were amber fire although the fury never showed on his expressionless face. "I trust that you will handle your tasks," he said. With that, he walked away with me next to him.

"Where are we going?" I whispered as we approached the entrance to Vita.

"You're going home where you'll be safe behind a ward. I need to visit Peter."

"I should go with you," I suggested. The proposal caused him to stop mid-step.

"What?"

"You'll get more out of him with me by your side. Your history with him won't do you any favors. My history with him might," I said, hoping that explanation would be enough and I wouldn't have to bring up that Dominic would never curry favor with a person whose kind he'd hunted and killed. Peter's mere presence seemed to strain Dominic's patience.

He studied me for a moment. "Afterward, you'll agree to go home?"

I nodded. Without magic, I would be more of a hindrance than an asset. Perhaps I could use that time to repair my tattered life.

The travel from Vita to the Underworld and then to mine left me slightly disoriented by the time we arrived in the parking lot of the condo Dominic shared with his sister. We headed straight to his SUV. A companionable silence lingered, with Dominic intermittently taking hold of my hand to deliver a kiss to it. Once he nipped at the skin, distracting me from any thought other than the previous night and this morning and how, no matter how chaste the intention of his touch, my mind always went straight to sex and magic. They were so entwined for me, I doubted they'd ever unravel.

"He's still dangerous to you," he reminded me as we pulled up at Peter's home. Peter was magicless and probably blaming me for it, so I was prepared for him to be hostile and erratic. After several minutes of knocking, we were greeted with a beleaguered and disheveled Peter. He was unrecognizable as the feared wielder of dark and powerful magic with plans to overtake and subjugate the supernaturals.

Without us having to request entrance, Peter moved aside to let us in. He appeared to have lost any instinct to protect himself. Live or die, he didn't care. His studious good looks were hidden behind a straggly short beard. He wasn't wearing his glasses, and his eyes looked unfocused. He was dressed in jeans and a wrinkled t-shirt that hung off him, but not in the casual aloof way as before.

"What?" he croaked, turning away from us and returning to his spot on the sofa. Books, loose papers with scribbling on them, and broken objects destroyed by him either in fits of anger or failed attempts of magic. Sigils on the walls and floor along with the burns in the hardwood made his living room look like the work of a desperate novice.

"Did your magic return?" Dominic asked, stepping in front of me and blocking my advance toward Peter.

"No," he hissed, looking down at the marking along his arm that appeared to have been drawn with black powder from the jar on the table. "Communication was severed, too. There's nothing." He lifted his eyes from his arm, a shadow of the person he was before.

"You were in communication with the person who took our magic?" I asked. This made the situation worse. Peter had thought he had an ally, only to be betrayed by them. It showed in the hollowness of his eyes.

He glared at Dominic with fiery anger that he'd have loved to act on if he had magic. For some reason Peter had assigned blame to him.

"You were just a pawn," Dominic asserted.

"I wasn't a pawn! I was the main part of the plan. I got into your world. I just—" He swallowed the rest, his lips pressing into a rigid line.

"Just what?" Dominic pushed through clenched teeth. It was obvious that Dominic was rarely so ill informed, and he wasn't handling it well. Peter responded with a defiant lift of his chin.

"Give me magic like yours," Peter said in a counter demand. "You want answers. What the Caster wants. What their plans are. Make me powerful again. Give me magic." He attempted to sound assertive, but it withered into a desperate plea. The room heated with Dominic's anger, and thirst for violence marred his expression.

"Luna, I need you to step out."

I didn't move. Couldn't move. Overwhelmed by the obligation to rein things in. With effort, Dominic turned to look at me. And I shook my head. He sucked in a breath, held it. When he blew out, I could see his failing effort to gain some semblance of control. His emotions had become a terrible navigator of the situation.

Dominic grabbed Peter by his throat, hoisted him in the air. The energy from his magic flooded the room. Color drained from Peter's face. I couldn't tell if it was because of Dominic's hold on him that seemed to be siphoning the life from him. Dominic had his mother's ability to create life, so why wouldn't the opposite be possible? The full range of his magic and cruelty was on display, claws extending from his free hand.

"How did you communicate with them?"

"Stop!" I yelled as the dagger-sharp claws came to his throat. Peter wilted under Dominic's hold. Dominic's cold, unapologetic eyes turned to me.

"This started with him," he provided through clenched teeth that didn't invite reasoning or challenge.

I was about to do both.

"A dead man can't answer any questions. He doesn't have magic and his failure has ensured that type of magic won't be returned to him." Then I turned my attention to Peter, allowing my eyes to freeze over enough that his eyes narrowed on me and his impassivity became insolence. "You need to help us. Your life doesn't have to end like this. Don't you want to make sure the person who betrayed you pays for it?"

The fleeting moment of defiance eked away.

Dominic dropped Peter who scuttled to the opposite side of the room. I followed and kneeled next to him. "Describe them?"

He shrugged. "We've never met."

He stood and opened a console. Pulling out a weathered leatherbound notebook, he handed it to me. I flipped through the blank pages.

"There's nothing here."

"I used to be able to make it appear. Not anymore. All communication has been severed. I can't find a way to reestablish it," he admitted, looking over the room that displayed his multiple failed attempts. He slumped back onto the sofa.

I ran my fingers over the pages in the same manner I had with the found book that started it all. Using me as a conduit for magic, the book had unleashed a spell that released the prisoners from the Perils.

The crisp edges cut my skin, and I let the blood that welled fall onto the pages, hoping I possessed enough remnants of magic that I could establish communication.

Nothing. Nothing more than a red-stained page. Dominic took the notebook from me and examined a few pages. Whispered something and waited. Several more attempts were made, but nothing was revealed.

Dominic stared down at the first page, examining it, seeing something I'd missed and continued to miss because the pages were still blank to me. "What was here?" he asked.

"Instructions," Peter said. Dominic's cold silence prodded him to elaborate. "On everything. The entire plan for us to return. I lived believing I was the only one. Settled down to the monotony of living an insipid life. One day, I came home to find the opened notebook and a spell next to it. I performed it and it revealed everything to me. Luna's existence, a strategy to use her to release the prisoners and provide us a way to gain entry to the Underworld—to the entirety of it, including the residences." Cold eyes turned to Dominic. "So that no one with power like yours could ever inflict your will ever again. You and yours should be dead. With the shades and Luna, things would have been different. You remained the roadblock we had to remove."

For a person hesitant to give information, he was now a broken dam of revelations, flooding us with intel as if it cleansed him. As if he could live vicariously through what could have been, despite his failure to execute it.

"I attempted the spell, but it failed." I suspected the very spells used to keep the prisoners from escaping saved the Underworld from being destroyed. His eyes lingered on me. "When it failed, I had no choice but to escape using a *temporalibus* spell. I wish it could have been another way. Our comparable magic made you the only person I could have used," he offered in explanation, a tinge of sympathy in his voice as if there wasn't a whole list of ruthless things he'd done to me that he should have apologized for.

I glared at him. His lips lifted in a wry, joyless smile. "You think I was wrong. I just wanted to right an injustice. You got his version of the story, which probably showed him in a favorable light, making them out to be the heroes."

Not one bit. I'd reluctantly accepted there'd be no heroes. Just a situation where one side was less wrong and horrific than the other, creating a circumstance where more people got to live and humans weren't reduced to a subservient role in society, or even worse, extinction. Perhaps not total extinction; vampires needed humans for food. But Peter had plans to rid the world of them, too.

"History is written by the victor. I can't tell you how many times I've heard you say that. Self-righteous touts offering their side of history and giving a voice to those who couldn't write their stories. Often citing that the victors are those who won not because they were better or more creative but rather the most brutal and amoral. You've spoken of that with disdain. Now you've become that person."

Pointing out the hypocrisy and forcing him to reconcile with the cognitive dissonance shattered something in him. His expression fell, emotion drained from his eyes, and he looked at Dominic.

Exposing his neck to Dominic, he whispered, "Do it."

What the actual fuck was wrong with everyone? Why was death always option number one?

"That's not the answer, dumbass!" Rude, but it snapped him out of it. He blinked several times before returning his attention to me. "Make things right," I went on. "You help us find the Dark Caster who stole our magic and who can now break the spells in the Underworld. I'm not confident they'll be able to destroy all the residents there. There will be survivors, and I can assure you that no one wants their new home to be here. Will you help us?"

Dominic's dark gaze bored into me, and when I met them the spark of fire blazed in them. I returned his sharp look, trying to convey that no good could come from his mother's creatures surviving and coming here.

Oh look, a bipedal panther! A congressional hearing and military action were definitely in the future if that occurred.

So much time passed while Peter deliberated, I expected him to make the death by claw request again. "It's not the innocuous supernaturals who are the problem," he finally said. "I believe they'll be safe from consequences. Those who rival their power are the ones they want to destroy." Dominic and Peter held each other's gaze. "They rightfully want to return the damage that was done to our kind."

"My actions are supported by the situation we're faced with now. Your kind chose to be unreasonable and indiscriminately dangerous. It needed to be done, so I did it. You're more rational and biddable because there are too few of you. But must I remind you of your plans when you thought you had Luna and the third Caster? You didn't expect the betrayal, nor your magic being stripped away."

Peter scoffed. "The people ruthless enough to rid the world of one danger have the audacity to label others too dangerous to exist?"

He's not wrong.

"You will help us? I'll do what I can to make things right," I promised, releasing any pretense that this was no longer my fight. It had fallen at my feet and something needed to be done about it.

Once again, the room plunged into an uncomfortable silence. "I want my magic back."

"No way in hell," Dominic retorted.

"We'll do what we can," I assured at the same time. Confusion moved over Peter's face as it became clear that Dominic and I didn't have a united front. When Dominic's steely eyes turned to me, I hoped he could figure out my intentions somehow. How could I tell him to agree but not make it a priority? It wasn't a no but fell squarely in my promise to do what we could.

"We will do what we can," he finally said, keeping his eyes on me. Either he was very perceptive or did what I hadn't and demonstrated our united front.

Peter's desolation transmuted into optimism. "I'll help you find the Dark Caster who stole our magic." That was his only priority now that there was the promise of having his magic restored.

Dominic pressed his hand into my back and guided me out the door.

"Where are we going?" I asked, getting into the vehicle.

"You're going home and I'm going hunting for shades. I will not allow them to be used as an army."

5

In a rush to get me home, Dominic was barreling through the traffic, taking speed limits as a suggestion, when he received an urgent call from Helena. With a hard set in his jaw, he made a U-turn in the middle of the street. I gathered from their back and forth that there had been an attack and the building where the Conventicle once met was no longer standing.

An entire building gone. Demolished. How the hell were they going to clean that up in a manner that wouldn't lead to a wave of wild speculation and think pieces that could possibly include magic? Convince the world the building had never existed? That was an unlikely solution. With the sighting of a werewolf on social media, and people who already believed in some variations of magic, the discovery of supernaturals seemed inevitable.

Helena directed us to a gray brick building. Dominic's eyes swept over the open space as he made his way to his sister and father who kept their distance from the occupants and maintained proximity to one of the two exits from the room. The abandoned warehouse that reminded me of a bunker was a decisive downgrade from the substantial space where the members of the Conventicle used to sit behind a semicircular table, the backdrop of the city visible from the floor-to-ceiling windows that took up the back wall. Now, they were in a large dank space with utilitarian metal tables, boxy complementing metal chairs, and simple recessed white lights that made the room look harsher. Since it was dusk, the room didn't have the assistance of the sun that could shine through the small, high, circular windows. Strewn throughout the room were an assortment of tools, as if the original occupants had left in a hurry. Bulk boxes that had been opened were in one corner.

Sometimes there's a miniscule silver lining to a disaster. The destruction of their building had unified the Conventicle and New Conventicle without any intervention from the royals. And based on the scowls directed at a small group of people whose heads were slightly bowed as if they'd been chastised, the disaster had led to changes in conviction. I recognized many of them although I didn't know their names. My attention was drawn to the Conventicle and New Conventicle members. I paid close attention to the one I was most familiar with, Emory, whose face remained impassive as he scanned the meeting area. The insolent dhole shifter made everyone cautious. It wasn't just the command he had over his shifting ability. Now, I was more wary of him because he'd survived a fight with Helena, during which she had slashed his neck with her claws. Dominic had warned us of who the tenacious shifters were, and the level of difficulty involved in killing one. Emory was proof of that resilience. Perhaps it was just him. It was hard to kill Emory.

His keen eyes turned to me, and my fight or flight instinct had me taking several steps back.

It might have been the destruction of the building that brought them together, but their mutual hatred of Dominic, Helena, and Areleus bonded them even more.

"What happened?" Dominic asked.

After being prompted, a man a few feet away spoke from where he huddled in a small cluster of people who were wearing similar looks of abject defeat. I assumed he was part of the Awakeners, which was confirmed once he spoke. His low, scratchy voice informed us that they had been approached by the Dark Caster, a woman who had no qualms about telling them her intention to destroy the Underworld and its occupants.

The tremble in his voice settled and evened out and he looked from Madeline to the trio of royals. "We had no problem with that. You have outlived your usefulness. I never felt you all should dictate how we live."

When I had been approached by one of the Awakeners, she'd made it very clear that by revealing their existence they would put in place plans for a hierarchical system where humans would be on the lowest rung. Once Dominic explained how their magic could do that with ease, I believed that could be our fate. Now, with the Awakeners aligned with the others, the Dark Caster's plans had to be worse than that.

"But you wanted to dictate how others lived," Dominic pointed out with a sneer.

It seemed that after the Dark Caster had stolen the magic from me and Peter, her first order of business was to destroy the Conventicle's meeting place. The second was to threaten the Awakeners into compliance.

Each breath I took was a struggle. Hopelessness crept in and none of the unsubstantiated confidence the people in the room were showing eased it. Coaxing myself into several measured breaths, I managed to control my brewing anxiety.

The best way to fix things was a plan that worked.

"Our way was the right way," the impertinent acolyte snapped. "But she didn't want that. It wasn't just your death that she wanted but that of anyone who didn't comply with her demands. There wasn't any reasoning or compromising with her. It was either her way or death." He swallowed hard. "She's powerful." Terror eclipsed his eyes and a frown marred his features. "It makes her bold in her demands and intention. You aren't a match for her. We managed to escape, but many of us are here because we don't want to die." The small group tightened their circle in a show of solidarity. "Your way is not what we wanted." He directed his eyes to the Conventicles. "We've chosen the lesser of two evils."

The Dark Caster's plans and tactics were making the case that Dominic's decision to rid the world of all of them wasn't as ruthless as it first appeared.

A woman stepped forward from the Conventicle's side of the room, moving with the effortless grace I'd attributed to vampires. "How did the prisoners escape again?" Her gaze immediately drifted in my direction. I knew I'd been assigned blame for this situation because I had been the beginning of it all. They didn't have irrefutable evidence, but nor did they need it. Their Seer, Callum, had implicated me and that was evidence enough. No one believed it was coincidence.

"We released them," Areleus admitted.

A harsh quiet fell over the room.

"Our problems weren't great enough that you deemed it necessary to release the people who want us dead? Your reason behind such a poor decision? Explain yourselves." Madeline, the self-appointed leader of the Conventicle, directed the question to the trio of royals.

"No." Areleus would never have to wonder why they hated him. He provided plenty of reasons while simultaneously making Dominic the more palatable of the two. "The only thing you need to know is once this is over, there will be requirements, of you all. Ones you will follow."

Dissension and anger swept through the room, and I felt

the brewing of more violence. The room came to a halt when the other Seer's voice rose over the grumbles.

"It doesn't matter what we agree to because you will fail. You and the human will die first," the Conventicle's tattooed Seer offered to Dominic. There was never warmness to his sights, just apathy and arid reporting. "Then you two next. The cruel one first and the other will follow."

The Seer's cryptic "cruel one" descriptor left me wondering if he was referring to Helena or Areleus. Taking the sneer that melded over his lips when he looked in Helena's direction, I figured it was her.

"That is what you see now. The end isn't definitive," Anand asserted as he entered the room. A confidence in his stride added a level of reassurance to his words.

Dominic stood taller at the appearance of his friend, and I wrestled with the urge to give Anand an overenthusiastic wave or a hug that he'd surely reject or that would make him downright uncomfortable. I didn't manage the same discipline when Nailah appeared next to him. Rushing to her, I pulled her into a hug. She stiffened but eventually relaxed into it, returning it with a warmth that I desperately needed. I didn't know if she was happy to see me, but she had to recognize the intention of the others and knew I needed an ally. With the exception of Dominic and Anand, I was in a room full of people who had wanted me dead at one point, still did, and were waiting for the opportunity to act on their wishes. I needed another person there who didn't want me dead and wanted to protect life as much as I did.

"You will be fine," she whispered. Her assurance should have eased my concerns, but it didn't. Absent from her prediction was the tell-tale violet glow of her eyes that indicated she was using her Seer gift. This was consolation and platitudes. Not the most practical thing but definitely what I needed.

"I hope you are right," the tattooed Seer countered without putting any effort into trying to sound sincere.

"Roman has been returned to the Perils," Anand announced, a disapproving frown bracketing his mouth when he looked at the ones who'd released him.

"And Celeste?" Madeline rushed out, making a noticeable effort to mask her panic. She didn't care about the fate of Roman or Vadim. Their lives meant nothing to her. Celeste had guaranteed that she wouldn't be the only person invested in her survival by magically linking her life to her bloodline. If she died, so did they. No one had been able to undo the spell.

Anand shook his head. "I can't find her."

"How do you plan to take care of this mess you created?" Madeline demanded of Areleus.

"It will be handled," Areleus offered with a level of unsubstantiated confidence that covered him like a bloom of fragrance and left me awestruck. "But I have requirements of you. Of all of you." His comfortably arrogant gaze roved slowly around the room, commanding their attention.

Madeline scoffed. "You make a mess and have requirements of us? We should be the ones demanding requirements."

"Perhaps you don't value your lives as much as you led me to believe." Areleus turned to leave, Helena close behind him. Dominic studied the collective panic surging over most of their faces. He charged at the door in a blur of movement, passing his father and sister and grabbing the figure beyond the door, pulling him into the room. He tossed the body across the room, sending the person crashing into the reinforced wall. Plaster fell but the wall stood. It was the vampire from the Perils. His graceful, liquid movements created shadows as he dodged Dominic's second strike, moving just out of reach. The stranger's movements were so swift I could only steal glimpses of his ash, low-shorn hair. From the reaction of the people in the room, I gathered who he was. Vadim. His parchment-color skin had a vibrant peachy undertone, presumably from a recent feeding.

Recovering from the attack, he moved with an intensity and blur of motion that I hadn't seen from other vampires. I didn't know if it was because he possessed different magic than typical vampires or because of his recent feeding, which gave me the eerie feeling that his victim hadn't been left alive. His preternatural speed made him flashes of movement. Tearing my eyes from useless attempts to track him, I searched the cluster of bodies that had moved away from the door until I found Nailah. I made my way to her while dividing my attention between Dominic and the others, who still viewed me as some variation of an enemy.

As I neared her, her violet eyes glowed briefly before fading to their gentle brown hue.

"Has he fed?" I asked.

She nodded.

"How many?"

"A lot. He's always possessed the adroit ability to cause the most damage in the shortest amount of time. Taking lives with the most amount of savagery." Her response was heavily laced with sorrow that leveled me with sadness and empathy and the wish that I could take some of the burden away.

Her frown deepened. "I couldn't see anything until we neared one of his victims. We weren't able to save them, and he fled. Anand spent too much time trying to save the person's life. It wouldn't have mattered. His determination to get the person he wants to harm the most meant I doubted even Anand could stop him."

No elaboration needed. Dominic had captured and imprisoned him. Apparently the only one who could. Vadim's vendetta was against the only person who could stop him.

He intended to exact his revenge and prevent it

happening again. With a vicious throaty rumble that sounded more feral than anything a human could produce, Vadim leapt into the air with shadowy movement, descending on Dominic with his outstretched poisonous claw-like nails ready to rip and tear into Dominic, rendering him magicless for as long as it remained in his system.

Dominic seemed reluctant to test the success of Helena's spell, dodging the claws at the risk of giving Vadim an advantage when he had to correct his position to keep from falling. Frustration flicked over Vadim's face as he lunged. Raising his hand, a surge of energy came from Dominic's palm that plowed the vampire back into the crowd, inches from me. Vadim risked a look in my direction, and his fury poured over me.

In his moment of recognition, I became his target. His hand lashed out to grab me. Lunging out of reach for the closest thing I could use as a weapon, I grabbed one of the tools left behind. A wrench. Heavy and well made. Vadim's grasp on my leg was met with me slamming the wrench down on his wrist as his hold on me tightened. His nails sinking into my skin caused me to cry out. Pain lanced through me. Another strike from me earned a simple sneer and a reminder of the level of pain they could endure. Before I could deliver more blows, Dominic was at my side, his claws slashing Vadim's wrist until he loosened his grip on my leg.

Dominic tossed him across the room, but with a display of preternatural speed and fluidity of movement, Vadim recovered from his fall. Despite his need to keep his eye on the real threat—Dominic—I garnered a great deal of Vadim's attention as he glanced several times in my direction, a covetous look spreading over his face each time. Dominic's vicious response to release me from Vadim's hold had exposed a weakness that he seemed determined to exploit.

He could retaliate against Dominic by using me. Dominic closed the distance between them. With a wave of his hand, he conjured a wall of fire, encircling the vampire and trapping him.

The vampire roared in frustration and rage and rushed through it. His clothes on fire, he changed course toward the crowd of onlookers. A goal to cause the most amount of damage. Madeline whispered a spell, and a rush of torrent energy that felt like a gust of wind but wasn't pulled from outdoors.

It smothered the flames. With claws and teeth bared, Vadim was a haze of movement barreling in my direction as I scrambled to get out of his line of sight. Dominic crashed into him, sending him back several feet, then raised his hands. A wave of energy surged from his palms, pushing the vampire back farther. In the burst of movement, I saw only a glint of the sword he'd borrowed from Anand's sheath. He struck the vampire with it. Beheaded him. Handed off the sword to Anand with the easy transition of an act done countless times. Then he approached the body that still managed to keep standing erect despite missing a necessary component. A resilience I couldn't imagine possible.

Dominic barely pressed his finger to the vampire's chest, and seconds later, his solid form became dust on the warehouse floor.

Some of the supernaturals were gaping as they looked at Dominic. They seemed to be getting reacquainted with him —the real Dominic. The man with a harsh, unrelenting set to his jaw, the burst of vibrant flames in his eyes that faded to reveal ruthless amber, and each step that marked a brutality that personified his very being. They had gotten used to the kinder version.

Madeline approached him in the manner one would a feral animal. Stilled when he moved, ignoring her and coming to me. Warmth crept into his expression as he placed a gentle hand on my arm.

"Are you okay?"

"Yes." He didn't relax until I lifted the wrench. "I was just about to kick his ass. Glad you got to him first. He wasn't ready for me."

"Your leg. I need to see it."

Pulling up the pant leg, he knelt to examine the angry red cuts. My leg throbbed, but since I didn't have magic to inhibit it, I was left with the secondary problem. Razor-sharp nails embedded in my skin.

His rumble of dissatisfaction filled the space. A hand covered the wounds, a cool feeling wrapped over them, dulling the fiery throbbing. When he removed his hand, he looked disappointed at the marks that remained.

"It'll heal," I said. His expression showed a need to retaliate. But Vadim was gone.

When he stood, I gave his arm a reassuring squeeze. "They're just small cuts. They'll heal in no time." I hoped I was right. If the nails were poisonous, could there be some aftereffect? I just hoped for the best. His fingers stroked my cheek, a soft comforting touch, but from the look he gave me, I suspected he wanted to do more but held back because of the audience.

"What?" he demanded through clenched teeth at Madeline, who'd inched closer.

Her voice was scratchy and soft, and absent was her typical aplomb and indignation. "Celeste cannot be handled in that manner." Whatever showed on Dominic's face when he turned to her drained the color from her face. "Please handle her with care. We need her alive. I believe we are close to finding a counterspell."

"I will honor the agreement I have with you." The apathy in his response didn't instill any confidence in the witches. Concern and fear were naked on their faces. He huffed out a breath. "Have I broken any contracts with you?" His steeled gaze held Madeline's.

"The prisoners were released," she countered.

"That wasn't my doing." They both lobbed acetic glances in Areleus and Helena's direction.

"They will honor it." The threat threaded through his words. He kept his eyes on the two. And perhaps the remnants of violence and anger were lingering from his fight with Vadim, but his presence felt like coiled violence ready to be released. He gave them a look that promised retaliation if they disobeyed.

Areleus and Dominic glaring across the room at each other ripped away any fleeting hope I had of a reconciliation between them. It would never happen. When this was over, only one of them would be alive. Their posturing and scowls made no secret of it. That was the known, as well as where Helena's alliance would fall in the aftermath.

Areleus tore his eyes from his son's. "Of course, your wishes will be honored," he said, donning a charming smile that hid the lecherous, power-hungry, untrustworthy lord. "That will be upheld. *However*, all other agreements must be voided."

A sly smile crept over Helena's lips. They were using this opportunity as a lever in preparation for Areleus to be the victor.

Unbothered, Dominic shrugged it off with an aloof smirk. "Do as you will. I will honor whatever is in place."

His chilly confidence made his father's expression morph into concern, tracking Dominic's every move with a heightened awareness. Predator to predator.

Emboldened by the obvious discord between Areleus and Dominic, Madeline's hubris had reasserted itself. "No changes to current agreements are needed. We will not return to you ruling us as if we were your subjects. Our autonomy is expected. We've had our share of problems, but they have been handled. We recognize that we must be more vigilant in squelching discord." She sent a scathing glance at the group of Awakeners, who dropped their gazes from hers like chided children. "The new directives will handle those who break them in a manner that will satisfy the new addition to the Conventicle." This was directed at the New Conventicles who shared their beliefs and wanted those who didn't comply to be met with violence or retribution that would coerce compliance. Her informal inclusion was met with smiles and nods of approval from the New Conventicles.

"Those who have sided with the Dark Caster?" Emory asked.

"They defected. They will be handled accordingly."

If they'd survived this battle, it would be for naught because they'd be punished by death. This was a cruel world that I desperately needed to abandon.

Listening to the exchange, I felt there was a level of undeserved self-righteousness.

Not to be that person. Screw it, I'm totally that person. The hypocrisy slayer. I had every intention of pointing out that by Madeline's logic, Helena and Areleus should receive the same punishment since they were the first defectors.

"The concessions that we made in the past will stand. We will not agree to more."

Areleus remained unfazed. "You will," he asserted in an unwavering tone that didn't invite further discussion.

Madeline clenched her jaw, aware that she had no basis for refusal because the royals were the only ones who could get them some semblance of normal by getting rid of the Dark Caster. But it would introduce a new normal, returning them to the royals' rule. No more autonomy.

Dominic pressed his hand into my back, guiding me toward the exit, with Anand close at his side. Dominic's withdrawal emboldened Areleus, who produced a contract that the supernaturals would be blood obligated to uphold. This was the part of their interaction that I welcomed and never wanted to witness again. After this issue was resolved, I hoped to emerge from my home to a world that was oblivious to all the creatures that went bump in the night... and the day.

6

Just as we made it out the room, a crash caused Dominic and Anand to stop and quickly return to the room. I stayed where I was, which gave me the vantage of seeing everything but not being part of it. The Seer who predicted our doom was crumpled in a heap on the floor, near the destroyed wall. Shades filed into the room along with a flurry of aggressive movement and magic. The unique sounds of shifters taking on their animal form soon followed.

One of the winged creatures was like a bird of prey, descending on one of the wolf shifters whose muscular body didn't hinder his ability to swiftly lunge out of the shade's way. The shade countered with a burst of magic whizzed at the creature to no effect. I wasn't sure whether in the shade's absence of being around shifters he'd forgotten their magic immunity, or whether it was something he'd try every chance he got, to determine if that had changed.

There were people with the shades. I gathered it was more shades who'd taken on human form. I had no idea why they would. Was it for the purpose of deceit, and was a human body a more adaptable form for fighting, allowing them to use the new form and magic to their advantage? Another shade in human form sped toward a vampire, who flashed its elongated teeth before charging. They crashed in a fury of strikes and punches before the shade, with a hip toss, landed the vampire on the floor. The shade placed his hand at the vampire's chest, like Dominic had done. The vampire convulsed several times and made a gurgled sound before he exploded into a puff of gray mist. I moved farther away, putting as much distance as I could between me and the violence and fighting, negotiating the flying bodies and aggressive magic, unable to determine who was winning.

As the fighting continued, it was too difficult to keep track of Dominic. Panic swept through me when I lost him. I searched the crowd and caught sight of Anand, who had given up hiding his magical abilities and was using it to corral the shades away from some of the supernaturals who were being overpowered. Those who knew him as a shifter now saw him as a being with the ability to control them. Instead of appreciation, I noted shock and apprehension from them; it explained why he chose to live with Dominic as opposed to living among them. Moving my attention from Anand, I finally found Dominic in the crowd. He was focused on a large man who'd drawn his lips back to expose his fangs. His attention quickly moved to the vampire's claws.

Emory, in his sleek, vicious animal form, caught a shade unaware and incapacitated it with his claws. It died in a macabre display of violence that drove me to look away. He turned the same demonstration of gruesome aggression on a witch acolyte of the Dark Caster. I stopped tracking Emory's whereabouts, slotting him into the category of those most likely to survive this.

Three menacing shades swooped in through a hole in the wall. One snatched up Emory with his claws. Dominic reacted with a magical spear that pierced through the crea-ture's body. It thrashed and writhed in pain as he set it ablaze with a fiery blast of energy, forcing it to drop Emory who plummeted toward the ground at an alarming speed. Quick to react, every movement of Dominic's hand guided him through the air with skillful precision, slowing his descent to a safe landing. Dominic then lashed out with fire at the creature's chest, resulting in an explosion of heat that burned the shade.

Anand moved forward with unrestrained ferocity, taking his assertion to heart that the royals and I wouldn't die, by intervening between the shade who'd set its eyes on me.

From my location just outside the door, I was in less danger of being hit by the hurling bodies, the indiscriminate firing of magic, or a wayward kick, elbow, or fist, but my panicked heartbeat wouldn't stop thrashing. It was necessary to stay on high alert. In the mesh of bodies on the floor and bodies launched through the room, I again lost sight of Dominic. Frantically scanning, I found him ending a fight with a vampire who'd sided with the Dark Caster.

Sorting through allies and enemies was becoming increasingly difficult. When I scoped a witch, vampire, or shifter, I wasn't sure whose side they were on. But I determined that consistently, if they were an enemy, they tended to be a vampire or witch. It spoke to the loyalty of shifters Dominic had told me about. They favored rules and order and were less likely to go against the others. And they must benefit the most from humans not knowing of their existence.

No one could deny that the impending victory was the result of having Anand and the royals with them. With the low numbers left of the Dark Caster's acolytes, I expected the allies to go for complete annihilation of any survivors, but when Madeline and three other witches came to a paralyzed halt, I wondered if they'd found empathy for their enemies. Terror and disbelief etched over their faces. I followed their eyes to the woman who'd emerged at the other side of the room. Not through a door or hole, just appearing, her energy changing the dynamics of the space, cascading through the area, drowning it in her immensity. The unique aura that accompanied Dominic and his family exuded from her. Distinctive, strong, and dominating. Celeste. Without the restraints of the spells that kept her imprisoned, the feel of her magic was visceral.

Squaring her shoulders added inches to her five-ten frame. Silver-blonde hair was twined in a French braid. Her striking features made determining her age difficult. She moved with a lithe grace, a smile inching across her face. She was a new and disturbing player in the game. With all the changing alliances and objectives, I had no idea what to expect from her.

The same dilemma flashed over the witches' expressions.

Celeste raised her hand and her mouth moved quickly, spitting out words, an illuminating ring forming around her as the door slammed closed. Tendrils of gray that I'd seen before, which pulled oxygen from the room, slithered and migrated at a steady, controlled rate toward the cluster of people. Despite her silence, Celeste's intentions were quite clear and expressed prolifically through her magic.

She wanted everyone dead.

Helena sped toward the enclosed witch. A silverish stream flowed from her and battered at the illuminated enclosure around Celeste. Her abrasive, haughty smile taunted Helena as the protective field held. The vampires didn't need oxygen; they would not be affected, but everyone else would.

Helena's petulance with denial of anything served in her favor. Determination fueled her. Her brow creased as she walked around the enclosure, studying it. Pressing her hand to it, occasionally gasping as she began to succumb to the magic that was drawing the air from the room. Witches worked to minimize its effect while struggling not to fall victim to it. Color leached from their faces, beads of sweat forming on their brows. Helena looked at Dominic and then at her father, and with a concerted effort a cyclonic wave of magic formed as theirs met, circling the enclosure, battering into it until it fell from Celeste. With an imperceptible explosion of movement, Helena's hands wrapped around Celeste's throat, claws out and seconds from making the kill despite Dominic's vocal objections. He was next to Helena, taking hold of the offending clawed hand and pulling the other away from Celeste's neck. From Celeste's pallid coloring, Helena was crushing her windpipe.

"You can't kill her," he gritted out.

"No, *you* can't. I don't care about the oath you made with them. She will die." The moment of discord gave Celeste the opportunity to move from their immediate grasp and display her adroit magical skills as she resurrected the barrier and pushed out the oxygen-depriving mist.

"They will all die. You all will." Her sweet melodious tone contrasted with her cruel behavior. The only thing I could determine was that Celeste was a magical sociopath whose actions were self-serving rather than on behalf of the Dark Caster. She wanted everyone dead. She locked eyes with a vampire whose confidence in his safety showed in his dark eyes.

Her taut lips lifted into a cruel smile. *"Verum mors."* I had no idea what it meant, but it struck fear onto the vampire's face. Another attempted to move but found her feet affixed to the floor. Panic was woven into every expression that moved over the vampire's face.

The royals went to work on removing the enclosure again but seemed to have more difficulty. Celeste was proving not only tenacious but adaptive, able to change the spell enough so the same tactics didn't work again. A confident smile bloomed as the mist crept over the room, presenting a greater challenge for the witches.

My mind was a buzz of bad ideas on how to help. I hated feeling so useless. My only option was to stay alive and do whatever necessary not to be a burden so no resources or magic would be directed to saving me.

Backing away from the mist that inched in my direction, I bumped up against a body behind me. I turned to face a woman whose curly, mahogany hair with reddish highlights was pulled into a low bun. Warm peach undertones gave her heart-shape face a pleasantness that belied the blaze of insistent urgency in her hazel eyes and the firm grasp she'd placed on my arm.

"Come," she ordered in a rushed whisper. Her hold moved from my arm to a firm cuff around my wrist, tugging me farther out the door. I rummaged through all the new faces I'd encountered over the weeks. Nothing about hers was familiar, but I couldn't tamp down the feeling that I'd met her before. Stumbling under her pull as she rushed me from the building, I yanked my wrist away once we had taken several paces.

"Who are you?" I demanded in a breathless huff, putting some distance between us. The amiable smile didn't waver, nor the staunch self-assurance, which I'd learned meant I was dealing with someone powerful.

"Help. Luna, I'm help."

Not a name nor an acceptable answer.

"What's help's name?" The question came out like a challenge because my internal alarms were telling me she wasn't the kind of help I wanted.

"Ophelia."

I doubted that was her real name and wondered if she'd given it because it was Greek for help, or twisted foreshadowing to a tragedy like Hamlet's Ophelia. Nothing about the choice seemed coincidental.

A smile tugged at her lips as she watched a shade in an upright position, using its wings to jump steps while he moved past us toward the warehouse. More people filing into the warehouse made her smile grow wider. I assumed it was the Awakeners. The reverent looks they offered her in passing quickly clued me to who she was. Like Peter, she'd been wrapped in an innocuous package.

Having the benefit of surprise as an advantage, I lunged at her. We crashed to the ground. Rolling her onto her stomach, I twisted her arm behind her back, shifting my weight to give me leverage and keep her secured against the ground.

"Stop," she whimpered in a voice so pitiful and pained, it gave me a moment of pause. She had to be. I wasn't wrong. This was the person who stole my magic. Killed the Awakeners who hadn't joined her or managed to escape.

She sobbed. "Let me go."

The second-guessing gnawed at me. The doubt was firmly planted. The treachery, switches in alliances, and betrayals had me questioning myself.

Listen to your gut, Luna. Something is off.

"I know who you are," I said, tightening my hold. "Do not play with me." Clearly, I'd been around violence too much because now my only thoughts were ending her and putting a stop to it all. Would her death send the shades back to the Underworld? What would dealing with a destabilized group of Awakeners be like? Could my life return to an imitation of normal where I'd pretend vampires, witches, shades, shifters, and other magical beings didn't exist? Where I believed the most dangerous thing to me was a person who thought the movie was better than the book?

An invisible tendril wrapped around me, ensorcelled in magic. It squeezed and sent a shocking pain through me. Tears blurred my vision, and my pained shriek continued to ring in my ear. She'd tossed me off her. As she attempted to stand, I swiped her leg with mine, sending her back to the ground with a shocked gasp of surprise.

People underestimating me worked to my advantage.

Straddling her, I attempted to secure her arms that were swiping wildly at me while a violent soundtrack of fighting in the warehouse commenced in the background.

Expecting a vicious retaliation that never came, I tried to think of a way to secure her. My scream for Anand with his exceptional hearing was cut off at the first syllable when my body seized in a fit of pain, an invisible vine coiling around my neck, applying enough pressure to allow just small wisps of breaths to seep through. The vine began to pulse, allowing full breaths before cruelly cutting them off. A display of skill and power. I didn't have magic, and if I did, wouldn't have honed it to any level to be a challenge to her. A flood of hopelessness came over me, but it was rapidly replaced by a burst of anger. Gathering all my oxygen-deprived strength, I punched her. Shock covered her face and the magic assault stopped. As a dark smirk worked its way to her lips, I responded with another punch that landed on her nose.

My first fight had been with one of the most dangerous and powerful beings in the world, and I hated it. Never wanted to do it again. I fought the urge to close my eyes to avoid seeing the blood spilling from her nose. The sight of blood shouldn't bother me, I'd seen so much of it lately, but it did, and I found some comfort in knowing that suffering still bothered me. Somehow, I managed to hold on to my humanity despite a deep-seated desire to pummel the woman under me. At least I could knock her out cold.

My third strike attempt. All traces of amusement and civility dropped from the mask she presented, mutating to a cold ominous steel that sent shivers through me.

"Now I'm debating if you're worth saving," she said, her voice matching the look she gave me. Magic in full force without a shred of mercy. A vice grip formed around my throat and body, crushing me. Immobile, I struggled for every breath. With magic, she tossed me off her.

On the ground, I struggled, clawing at the magical vine

around me. There was nothing to grab. I needed to stop the source. The Dark Caster stood, squared her shoulders, coming to her full height. A portentous presence. A golden halation flowed from her and covered me. I battled the darkness that threatened to take over. With a last-ditch effort, I grabbed her before collapsing.

The blackness receded. She wasn't trying to kill me—just subdue me. That was more troubling because obviously she viewed me as of use to her. Not disposable right then, but her casual display of power was a reminder that if I was no longer of value, she could easily dispose of me.

"Ansel—" Her lips turned up in disgust. "Peter—he is deserving of his human name—

proved to be useless. You've spent time with Dominic, Helena, and Areleus and," her brow cocked, "their mother. Have you meet Ileana?"

That was my use. Information.

My lips tightened in a painful thin line to ensure not one bit of information escaped. Sneering at my resistance, she placed a hand on my shoulder and a jolt ran through me. I wailed. The sound hung in the air. Her dark smirk widened.

"Have you met Ileana?" There was desperate longing in her interrogation.

When I didn't answer, she delivered another painful jolt that wracked my body. Constant and unrelenting. Tears blurred my vision.

"Stop, please," I said between the choked gasps. "I can't think."

"You have to think about whether you've met Ileana?"

My lips returned to the rigid line. She huffed a breath, and with a wave of her hand, it all stopped. My breathing normalized and I took several deep ones, my body craving oxygen. Pain. I had felt it so much lately, I didn't respond typically to the relief.

Slowly I hauled myself up, furtively scanning for weapons

or help. Nothing and no one was available. With magic and shades at her command, she had a definite advantage. Could I outrun her?

"Why?" I asked. The question served as a distraction from the one she wanted answered.

"Why what?" A spark of interest lit her eyes.

So many questions ran through my mind. All of them begging to be answered. *How did you stay hidden for so long? What happens if you destroy the Underworld? Why was I chosen to hold Dark Caster magic?*

"Why are you doing this?" Perhaps it was the unintended pitiable way I asked that led to her stern look of contempt easing.

"We were hunted and destroyed. There can be no other reason. Revenge."

I heard the "and" in her words. There was no finality to it.

"And?"

"Destroy the Underworld and those in it."

"And the people here, what will happen to them? Will they be destroyed as well?" There had to be some lingering bitterness toward them. They didn't commit the offenses; they were avid supporters of it. "Do you believe magic shouldn't exist here?" Her eyes brightened at my question, and I heard it also in my words. Fear, panic, fatigue, and raw and abject helplessness laced my question. It falsely led her to assume our goals aligned.

"I don't want to end all magic. I strive for order. I will provide that so that we can coexist with the humans without issues. My magic will ensure compliance."

"Not from everyone. Shifters are immune to magic."

That excited sparkle renewed itself. "Shifters will be divested of their immunity. There can't be order if they maintain that advantage. Too many vampires currently exist. It is a hassle. Those that can integrate the best in this new world will be spared. If Celeste succeeds, that makes things much easier for me. If she doesn't, it is still an advantage. If she is killed, the strongest witches, those who would prove to be a problem for me, will die. If her life is spared by Dominic and his family, I will step in to remedy that lapse in judgment." Her eyes migrated to the building where Celeste was either being defeated or killing any threats to the Dark Caster. She might not be an ally, but she'd become an unwitting accomplice.

Ophelia's horrid plans mirrored Peter's but came with a side of what-the-fuck-this-is-horrible-beyond-imagination.

From her wistful look she was waiting for accolades, a pat on the head, or some form of compliment. I just wanted to punch her again. Did the Awakeners realize they were helping the very person who planned to destroy them?

An Oscar-winning actor wouldn't be able to hide their abhorrence at her plans. I failed miserably at hiding my sheer disgust.

Her delight withered. Glaring at me, she opened her palm. Magic tugged at me, pulling me closer to her. Just as she was about to reach for me a blast smashed into her back, hurling her at a tree several feet away. Helena's eyes blazed with fire. The fire diffused into amber. Taking in the situation, she seemed to gather what she'd just saved me from. The menacing promise of consequences were in each step Helena made toward Ophelia.

Another mass of magic whizzed past me to Ophelia, hitting the tree where the Caster had been. She was gone. We both searched. I expected a quick reappearance and willingness to challenge Helena. There wasn't. Instead, the remaining shades fled from the building, as did the Dark Caster's acolytes, of whom there were notably fewer.

"Luna, are you okay?" Helena's urgent question broke through the noise. A harsh whooshing stopped my response. The space where Helena stood was now empty.

Scanning the area, I called for her despite knowing she'd never respond.

Then I called Dominic. He was at my side before his name could fully leave my lips.

"What?" he rushed out, his hands on my shoulder in a desperate attempt to give me his full attention and ignore the activity behind us.

"The Dark Caster was here. She took Helena." I explained everything that happened. He kept me close at his side as we rushed back into the building. Celeste was gone but Madeline standing among the ruins keyed me in that Celeste was still alive. Their bloodline was protected for now. I skimmed over the sickening evidence of the war and the smaller number of people who still occupied the room. I let the naïve thought that they'd left voluntarily creep in, and not the chilling reality of what actually occurred.

"Finish up here," Dominic directed Anand. He explained Helena's disappearance to Areleus, tasking him with initial efforts to find her.

"Where are you going? Your sister is missing," Areleus hissed when Dominic turned his hand lightly on my elbow, guiding me toward his SUV.

"Taking Luna to safety. I'll join you when I return."

"You will do no such thing," he roared. "Finding Helena takes priority. Your—" His preferred use of *human* wasn't what came to mind, and the spiteful look hurled at me was proof.

"Both are a priority. I've lost my sister. I won't lose Luna."

I despised the sorrow in his tone whether his father caught it or not. It wasn't primarily her abduction—it was her betrayal that festered, and yet he couldn't stop being concerned about her. The warring emotions had to be difficult to manage.

He moved closer to his father, dropping his voice to a whisper and ignoring the buzz of discussion about the Dark

Caster's presence and Helena's abduction. The group didn't seem concerned about Helena being missing and wouldn't be easily persuaded to do anything about it.

"You need to form a search party. Convince them of the importance of finding Helena. At this moment, the only thing they care about is the Caster's involvement."

I wasn't confident that Areleus would be able to do it and that searching for Helena would be left to them.

Not giving Areleus an opportunity for further debate, and placing his hand on my back, Dominic steered me toward the SUV.

"I don't want to go to the Underworld or your mother's realm," I blurted out once in the car.

"It wouldn't be safe for you there anyway. If Ophelia has Helena, she's probably looking for an entrance there. I don't believe you're a priority now that she has her, but you're still a target. I won't allow you to be an easy target."

So many people hated me and blamed me for things, I didn't bother to ask. The only person I'd trust would be Dominic and Anand. In my opinion, even Ileana was suspect.

Dominic remained distracted while he navigated toward my apartment, probably worrying about Areleus's ability to persuade them to look for Helena. Charging next to me was the phone Dominic had retrieved from the glove compartment and given me to replace mine. I had no idea when I'd lost my phone. The last time I was sure it was with me was when I attempted to steal Peter's magic. If that was when it was lost, I was positive it had been destroyed. There wasn't any doubt that the anger and wrath he felt for me was enacted on my phone. But I'd erase my information nevertheless.

A concerned look marred Dominic's features. He was burdened with the same conundrum that most siblings experience. Angry with their sibling but adhering to the rule that no one else could ever hurt them. It was solely the domain of other siblings. Despite threatening to kill her hours ago, preventing her ending Celeste and thereby ending an entire bloodline of witches, he'd do whatever was necessary to find her.

What benefit did the Dark Caster see in taking Helena? How would she use her against the royals and Ileana? Helena possessed her own powerful magic, was a skilled fighter, and her explosive temper was just a cross word from being detonated. She craved power and her loyalty was tenuous, but I didn't believe she'd destroy her whole family and the realms of the Underworld to attain it.

Emoni's head snapped up from the book she was reading on the sofa, when I opened the door. A weekender and smaller bag were housed in the corner of the room. A cup of coffee next to her. She'd made herself at home, or as much as she could while waiting for me. The crease of worry was the first thing I noticed about her.

"Hi," her small voice offered as she pulled out the key explaining her presence. At my approach, she exhaled a soft, ragged breath, relief smoothing out her frown. It was quickly restored at the sight of Dominic.

"I've been here since you left to visit your family for dinner because I hadn't heard from you since then." Her gaze returned to Dominic. "My worries don't seem to be a priority for you these days."

The pain in her voice was palpable, overshadowing the tinge of anguish. It felt like a gut punch. It had to seem like I'd abandoned her and stopped caring about her feelings.

"It's been a really rough couple of days." My voice broke. She stood up and stiffened, as if forcing herself not to offer comfort or let me off the hook. She wanted answers. She deserved answers. Emoni had a hard time averting her eyes from Dominic, to whom she'd definitely attributed blame. The cold ire in them had no effect on him. Often on the receiving end of hostility, he'd developed an immunity to it.

"That's on me," Dominic provided, cool and devoid of emotion. It was a statement, not a request for forgiveness or understanding. Things happened and he would not offer any excuse for it. Emoni had no intention of offering anyway.

"We're not friends," she shot back at him, obviously not in a mood to be placated by his ownership of responsibilities. Dragging her eyes from Dominic, she fixed them on me. "We are."

The hurt in her voice broke my heart. If the roles were reversed, I would have been sick with worry, and disappointed, too. And that's what was happening. It showed in her deflated expression, the glisten of unshed tears in her eyes, and her burdened posture. I was responsible for it. What had it been like for her the past few days?

"You're right. I'm so sorry." Pulling her into a hug, I whispered a promise. "I'll tell you everything. Not the abridged version. Everything."

Turning to Dominic, I nodded for him to go. Even at my urging, he seemed reluctant to leave.

"Go," I pressed him. "Find Helena." Nothing he said would make things right with Emoni, so I'd have to do my best. He moved toward me, cupped my chin in his hand. Warm lips covered mine, his tongue entwining and exploring mine with a ravenous hunger and a promise to continue. Delicious heat coursed through me. When he pulled away, I felt his absence and his commanding presence.

Only a beat of time had passed. Knowing the drill, I pulled a strand of hair and gave it to him.

Emoni scrutinized the exchange. "What are you going to do with that?" she asked.

"A ward. It is linked to her and she's the only one who can break it." Dominic went on to explain the rules and limitations of the ward.

"If I do the same, can it be linked to us both, preventing her dismantling it without me?" She gave me a look that dared me to challenge her request. Her expression was hopeful as she moved her hand to her hair.

"I can't do that."

"Can't or *won't*?"

"Can't." His response was clipped as he fought his irritation dealing with a rightfully worried Emoni.

"Can you make a ward that would keep us here and prevent us leaving?"

"Imprisoning—"

"It's not imprisoning her. It's regulating her departure," she quickly refuted.

Sounds like imprisoning to me.

Dominic's patience was faltering. With jaws clenched, he forced his words through gritted teeth. "Semantics don't matter. She would still be imprisoned and that's *not* the safest thing for either of you. I don't anticipate anyone coming for her. But it would be foolish to believe that she is no longer a person of interest for many."

Person of interest prompted Emoni into protective friend mode. "Hurry and put it up, please."

His reluctance to leave was obvious. "Stay here unless it's no longer safe to do so." He inhaled a breath, displaying the intense withdrawn look he got when he was analyzing a situation and trying to determine the best course of action. How easy the situation would be if he could dismiss Helena's life with the same ease she'd dismissed his.

"I may send Anand here, but I need him for a while."

"I'll be fine," I said.

He nodded, erected the ward, and closed the door.

I had displayed more bravado than I'd felt.

"We will be fine," Emoni piped up in a spirited voice, trying to allay the unease that must have shown on my face. With an encouraging sympathetic smile, she moved to the corner and picked up the smaller backpack and dropped it in front of the sofa. She plopped onto the sofa and invited me to sit next to her. Opening the backpack, she proudly revealed an assortment of gadgets, weapons, and other accoutrements for protection.

"I brought these just in case things got truly terrible." The tight smile dipped into a frown. "I feel like we're there."

At the top of the heap of weapons and gadgets were zip ties.

"What were you going to do with these?" I asked, snatching up the bundle.

"I had no idea what was going on. Was it going to be a rescue mission or an escape?" In response to my confusion, she blew out an exasperated breath. "Okay, I didn't have a concrete plan, but someone was going to be tied up. They need their hands for magic, so I was going to prevent any use of magic. You can't shift if you're bound. I'm not sure how'd I deal with vampires, but I have this." She pulled out a vial of what I assumed was holy water, several surprisingly well-made stakes, and handmade wooden crosses. "The holy water was blessed by Pastor Tanner. That bastard actually charged me for it."

"Of course he did. He has a divorce lawyer to pay," I pointed out. Tanner was a disgraced pastor from the local nondenominational church who'd risen to fame when his mistress and their three children were discovered. "If he blessed it, how holy do you think that water is?"

I didn't pursue a conversation on how she'd convinced him to do it. *Hey pastor, can you bless this water so I can go fight vampires?*

"I was not in a position to be picky. Desperate times. He still has the church. I assume a hypocrite's blessing is better than none. I'm prepared for it all." She was so confident in her arsenal, it was heartbreaking to dispel her beliefs.

"Shifters are really strong. They'd break the binding during their shift. Holy water and crosses are a myth. You stop a vampire by driving a stake through their heart or cutting off their head. They're ridiculously fast and strong. Without the element of surprise, a human is unlikely to be successful at doing that. And they can disappear. If they feed, then your efforts were for nothing. I'm not confident witches need their hands for all magic. Sometimes the magic is in the form of a spell and can be just as dangerous." I'd became a wealth of super-natural information—something I wasn't particularly proud of. I recalled the ease with which Ophelia used her magic. Without lifting a finger, she'd subjected me to unspeakable pain.

Emoni's frown deepened but she didn't look discouraged. She presented a massive knife that could do serious damage, but I was more concerned the damage would be to her.

"Do you know how to use that?"

"I know how to debone a chicken."

"You think a magic wielder is going to stay still and let you debone them?"

"I was desperate." She pouted playfully. "Stop punching logic holes in my vampire slayer and magic assassin fantasy," she grumbled.

"You're right. I'm confident you would have come with your arsenal of weapons and your knife ready to slice and dice in order to help me," I teased.

She rolled her eyes and sank into the sofa.

"Where have you been? What happened?" she asked.

"It's a lot," I warned.

The scowl twisted her pleasing features. "How much alcohol will I need?"

Flashing a weak smile, I went to the kitchen and rummaged through my cabinets and pulled out a bottle of vodka.

"Probably this. Straight," I said, pushing humor into my voice that I knew wouldn't soften anything I was about to tell her.

Emoni got the whole story, from being attacked by Conventicles, Helena and Areleus's betrayal, me saving Dominic by slamming a car into them. I paused while Emoni took another shot after being told that hitting them with a car didn't kill them.

"You might want to pace yourself. It gets weirder." Once I'd told her about meeting Ileana, her creatures, and becoming one of her created with magic, Emoni shoved the bottle in my direction.

"I think this should be for you."

I rejected the offer, and she appeared to lose the desire for it, too. The information was so sobering, alcohol couldn't dull it.

"Is the mom as terrible as her daughter and husband?" Emoni frowned, I suppose recollecting her meeting with them. They hadn't left a good impression.

"They weren't married. They just wanted to customize their children," I admitted, her question prompting me to tell her about the reason for Helena and Dominic.

"Everything about these people is calculating and dangerous. You don't need to be involved. Nothing good can come of it." She sighed. "I don't think he's worth it. None of this is worth it."

It was like my heart felt the need to remind me how much I cared about Dominic, because the mere thought of walking away left emptiness that I wasn't sure I could handle.

Not addressing her comment, I continued, revealing Peter and my magic being stolen, Helena's releasing the worst prisoners, the Dark Caster's plans, and Helena being taken when my abduction was unsuccessful.

Emoni pulled me into a tight hug as if she feared I was moments from being snatched away. The load felt lighter after telling it to her, but I felt guilty, knowing it was a burden we now shared. Her phone buzzed, pulling her from the hug. Grabbing her phone off the coffee table, she looked at it.

"It's your brother," she mumbled, then answered the video call with a tight grin and told him that I was right beside her.

Without further discussion, she quickly passed me the phone.

"Hey." I made my tone light and airy. *Not a trouble in the world.*

"What the hell do you mean *hey!*" he growled, a streak of pink running along his cheeks and the bridge of his nose.

"Give me a minute, I need to grab something," I lied. I muted the phone and turned off the camera to keep him from reading my lips. "What does he know?" I asked Emoni.

"Nothing. He's been calling and texting me since your disappearance, but I avoided them all. I sent him a text to let him know I'd contact him as soon as I heard from you. I didn't want to lie, but I damn sure wasn't going to tell him the truth." She frowned. "I didn't really know the truth, did I? Things are so different than what I was expecting." She cast her gaze downward. Perhaps looking at me reminded her of how she felt being in the dark about everything.

Taking a slow measured breath, I released it while unmuting the phone and turning on the camera. "Forest—"

"Are werewolves real?" he blurted.

8

"**W**hat?"

It was the only thing I could manage. My mouth bone dry, I picked up the glass of water and gulped half of it. I heard his question but it shocked me into silence. Emoni had relayed that social media had been inundated with reports of a werewolf sighting that created a whirl of speculation about the existence of magic and its creatures. Since all evidence of the video had disappeared with the help of a techno-witch and the supernaturals having implemented processes they'd used in the past to remain hidden, I thought Forest's curiosity would have been squelched. That day, I did my part to downplay the alleged sighting. Forest's interests tended to be fleeting. I left my parents' home believing I had successfully convinced Forest that werewolves were just an entertaining idea. I was wrong.

"You heard me, Luna." His usual playful, breezy demeanor was gone. His tight, jagged voice was the result of a restless worry. I couldn't imagine how unsettled he was, speculating whether magical creatures existed. His brows knitted together as he waited for me to answer.

Since he hadn't modulated his voice, Emoni could hear

the conversation. Her stern, earthy brown eyes locked on me, awaiting my response. The answer was stuck in my throat. Even if I managed to say something it would be a jumbled mess since I hadn't sorted the stream of thoughts running through my mind.

I sighed and picked up my glass of water again. Withholding information and skirting around the truth was getting to me. Could Forest handle the knowledge that magical beings lived alongside us, albeit unnoticed? People always believed in their self-resilience and ability to handle almost anything. And Forest had always been optimistic and open minded, but this might be too much for him.

"No," I managed. Emoni's jaw dropped before she ushered the shock away and replaced it with a scowl of disapproval.

"You're a terrible liar. Not only can I hear it in your voice, but I can see it in your face, Luna," Forest scoffed. Being an adept liar wasn't something to be proud of, but I thought I was adequate at disguising the truth. But not from my brother, who knew me too well.

While I debated how to respond, Forest eliminated the need to come up with a convincing lie. "I saw you. *And them.* The man being stabbed by the claws. You running those people over with the car. And another man disappearing. There were things that definitely weren't human there. Don't give me any bullshit excuse about it being costumes, make-up, cosplay, or any other sort of make-believe. I know what that looks like and what they can do, and this wasn't anything like it. Luna, I need the truth." It wasn't a request but an order.

I couldn't breathe. Disclosing the information meant I was putting another person I loved in danger.

"I'm coming over there," he said.

"No!" Emoni had joined my objection. Him coming over meant I'd have to break the ward to let him in.

Telling him the truth and withholding information both

filled me with anxiety and dread. Each action had reper-
cussions.

"It's...complicated," I whispered so softly that Emoni
moved closer so she wouldn't have to strain to hear me.

"I saw things...things that aren't supposed to exist," Forest
said, his voice heavy with confusion and angst.

The tension in the room could have been cut with a knife
between Emoni and I. Because she had been on the other
side of the fabrications and lies of omission, I knew she was
reluctant to have the same done to Forest. Emoni broke the
silence.

"Luna, tell him."

I swallowed hard and tried to determine how to reveal
the information. There wasn't a way to sugarcoat it or
deliver it in a way that wasn't troubling.

"Secrecy is important to them, and they go to great
lengths to maintain it," I said, gravity threaded in my words.

"I gathered that. When you left, I wasn't too far behind,
but when I approached, I felt an unease and didn't want to go
in that direction. Something didn't sit right with me. Your
demeanor was off when I told you about the video, and you
seemed anxious to leave. Anytime I moved closer, I got a
sickening feeling. Weird anxiety and fear over nothing.
Everything just felt wrong. I took another route. Parked and
moved toward the nature reserve. I saw a man turn into a
wolf..." His voice trailed off as if he was trying to assure
himself that his eyes hadn't betrayed him. "I had to use my
phone to get a better look because every time I approached
the area, those strange feelings would hit me again."

"It was a spell to repel people," I provided.

"Magic," he whispered.

"Yeah."

"I didn't see everything, but enough. I saw enough. And
glimpses of you. When you disappeared with that...that...
man?" There wasn't certainty in his use of the descriptor

"man" because Forest knew Dominic was more but had no idea what.

"You have a video?"

"No. I couldn't get it to work."

If nothing else, techno-witches were efficient and by far the most essential member in maintaining their secrecy.

"Forest, I'm going to tell you everything. And then you must behave as if you know nothing. Don't investigate. If you suspect someone is off, not quite human, don't let on that you do. Leave it alone." If the magnitude of the danger wasn't infused in my voice, it was definitely in my face.

"I know."

He was given all the information while Emoni sat in silence, an indecipherable look on her face. The emotionless mask she wore didn't provide any feedback on whether I should change my delivery. Did I need to soften, ease him into it? He'd seen it. Nothing could be more traumatizing than seeing that unprepared. I knew from experience. So, I opted to be candidly direct.

"Am I like you?" he asked. Horror had swept over his face when I told him of the discovery of the mark on me.

"No. I checked."

Realization lifted his lips into a smirk. "I knew there was more to you being so overly affectionate that day at dinner."

"No, I meant it. It had dual purposes. I missed you!"

The boom of laughter was infectious even if I knew it was a response of learning the horrid information and the betrayal of my mother's friend. I continued filling him in on the rest of the information.

"You died!?" Of course, I couldn't slip that in as an afterthought. Ileana recreating me wasn't something minor. For a brief moment, I'd had magic. Wielded power that contended with some of the most powerful beings. It was so short-lived, and I couldn't believe I actually missed it. It wasn't the magic. Nothing compared to the confidence I felt having the ability to truly protect myself.

"Not really," I said.

"Sounds like you did. I'm not sure why you keep brushing over it like she did some minor spell and bam, you were a magical entity or whatever. You were made into a new person," Emoni piped in from the sidelines. I could have done without her commentary.

"I'm the same person."

"Now. Because your magic was stolen." Her interjection opened the door for me to proceed to tell Forest about my interaction with the Dark Caster and her proposal. The ball that had settled in my chest tightened at my brother's calm demeanor. Had he descended into a fugue state? His glassy eyes connected with mine before he closed them and took a deep breath.

"Gloria was a Dark Caster?" he asked.

"We're uncertain. She was either a Dark Caster or an acolyte. I believe there are some humans that aren't as oblivious to the existence of the supernaturals as they'd like to believe. Nevertheless, I was a contingency plan."

"You need to get out of there. Come stay with me or our parents."

I explained the ward to him and that I was safest in my apartment.

"Emoni's with you, too?"

"Not by my doing or desire," I said.

"Hey! Harsh," she blurted.

"I'm not trying to be, but you realize if I could have protected you from this, I would have. The more people at risk, the more difficult things are for Dominic."

"Dominic." Forest said his name with a hint of aversion. He'd definitely attributed him to being the problem.

"He was just doing his job. Don't blame him. If anyone is

to blame, it's Gloria. If I'd never been given the magic and marked, none of this would have happened."

"What can I do to help?" he asked. I knew telling him to do nothing wouldn't sit well with him, but that was the only thing he could do.

"Keep this information a secret and go on with your life as usual. Anything else would be suspicious." I took out the phone Dominic gave me and sent him a text message so he'd know how to reach me. It eased the crease of worry on his face.

"Don't worry. This will be over soon and everything will go back to normal."

"Normal?" He didn't believe that for one moment.

I shrugged. "As normal as it can be."

"Don't let anyone do anything to me," he blurted.

"Like what?"

"Take my memories. If they're able to erase videos and prevent recordings, I'm sure a person's fragile mind isn't hard to fuck with."

"No one will do anything to you. If they try"—I turned the phone toward Emoni's bag—"they'll have to deal with Emoni and her bag of weapons."

He was frowning when they came into view. Brow raised, his eyes migrated to the side, hoping to get a glimpse of her. I wondered if he was trying to imagine Emoni's vision of herself as the kick-ass, weapon-wielding vigilante.

"Does she know how to use any of that?"

"I'm assuming she knows how to use zip ties. And our Lady of Wrath and Fire informed me that she can debone a chicken, and apparently that's all one needs to fight shifters, vampires, and witches. Well, that's what she believes." I grinned at Forest's thundering laugh, fully aware of Emoni's intense glare drilling into the side of my face.

"Okay, now that I know you're truly safe, I'll worry a little less." He wouldn't. We said our goodbyes, but before we ended the call, he said, "Answer my texts. No matter what. I need to know you're okay."

It was the only compromise he'd give me, and I knew if I missed any messages, he wouldn't abide by his agreement. It was understandable. If things were different and he was the one providing this information, I'm not sure I'd be as generous and understanding.

I agreed.

9

$\mathcal{A}$n hour since the ward around my apartment had been placed and Dominic had left. Worry crept in and settled over me. Without a way to contact him, I began to think the worst. I didn't think things would be resolved quickly, but I wanted to know about any progress. And I was worried about him.

I tried distracting myself with a book but couldn't focus enough to get into the light, cute rom-com. Previously, an adorable main character and a grumpy love interest would have effortlessly held my attention. Now, it simply reminded me that there wasn't anything quirky or lighthearted about my life at the moment.

And I couldn't take any steps toward mending things with my job. Emoni had confirmed what I already knew: I didn't have one. She discouraged me from contacting Cameron, the store owner.

"It's better to do that face to face when everything is over, or at least controlled enough that you won't have the threat of your life being upended again. If by some chance she allows you back, I doubt she'd give you a second chance."

Emoni was right. But I needed a distraction.

"When is your next gig?" I asked.

She excitedly told me about her next bookings and how it was heartbreaking to find out that one of her songs became a sound on TikTok and that I'd missed it.

Hearing that, I'd never wanted to walk away more. Just say screw it to all of it—and force them to accept that. This wasn't my fight and I should be able to bow out. Power-hungry people wanting a civil war shouldn't mean I had to miss my friends' successes and not be there to celebrate with them. The insistence on secrecy. Me stumbling into the middle of it just because of a series of unlucky events. It wasn't all bad, though. In the chaos, deplorable situations, and violence, I'd found something special with Dominic. Initially, I thought it was just physical, but it was more than merely amazing sex with a gorgeous man. I was a priority to Dominic, whereas with my ex, Jackson, I was often treated as an afterthought. The effect the royals' decisions had on human life hadn't meant much to Dominic before, but now it was a consideration. I adored the way I felt when he was near, when he touched me. Even the way he looked at me. I wanted him in my life. That reason alone kept me from trying to figure out a way to burn it all to the ground so I could have my old life back.

Reluctantly, I pushed aside the fantasy of ending this, because fantasy is all that it was. I was left with the guilt of a worrying brother, sharing in my best friend's successes days too late, and feeling like an observer rather than an active participant in my life.

The lump in my chest grew, and as Emoni enthusiastically retold the event, sadness crept in.

"What's with the face?" she asked.

I shook my head, the words caught in my throat. It took several moments before I could speak. "I'm sorry I wasn't there to share that with you."

She smiled. "You're acting like it won't happen again. It

will. And you won't be dealing with Underworld realms, wars, and weird creatures of the night—or is it day—or whatever. Creepy magicals that live among us."

Emoni expelled a whoosh of breath when I pulled her into a big hug. "You're the best friend a person could ever ask for," I whispered into her ear.

"I know," she whispered. "I should get some type of commendation," she teased.

When Emoni had run out of news and I was left alone with my thoughts, worry reared its ugly head, so I tried distracting myself by cleaning my apartment and occasionally paying attention to the subtitles of a drama that had captured Emoni's attention. But my mind kept slipping into listing all the things that could go wrong. Emoni pulled her attention from the tv and scrutinized me.

Offering me a weak smile, she said, "No news is good news, right?"

"When has that ever been true?" I challenged.

"I know." She squeaked out of a weird excitement in our shared belief. "That's the worst platitude, isn't it? You're going to hate me for saying this, but you will have to wait and deal with it. What's the alternative?"

She was right. Nodding, I abandoned cleaning and plopped down next to her.

"Let me see the synopsis and catch me up." She was more than happy to catch me up on the enemies-to-lovers college drama.

The show was distracting enough that I startled at the abrupt, commanding knock at the door. Expecting Dominic, I rushed to it, only to find his mother.

I silently mouthed to Emoni who it was. Her expression was an amalgamation of fear, curiosity, doubt, and the need to escape danger at the idea of meeting her. Glassy eyes seemed to be recounting all the things I'd told her about Ileana. The desire to flee overrode the other emotions.

Ileana's otherworldly appearance stood in stark contrast to the urban environment outside my apartment. Seeing her without the backdrop of verdant trees and forestry, vibrant flowers, and her peculiar creatures roaming about was uncomfortable, and her discomfited appearance showed it. Wearing a flowing satin gown that shifted and shimmered in hues of violet and silver, her commanding presence evoked the diametric feeling of fear and draw. Unlike the royals, she didn't seem capable of managing some semblance of assimilation. Her command of the space was undeniable.

"Ileana," I whispered with an attempt to add as much reverence as I could.

Emoni pulled me from the door, grasping my wrist in what was either a show of solidarity or an urgency to run like hell. Her grip on me tightened as annoyance washed over Ileana's face when the ward illuminated and prevented her entering. Pressing her hand to it, she whispered a few words, her expectant look disappearing when the ward remained intact.

"The ward." Her crisp voice requested the removal. I had to pry myself out of Emoni's grip, who would have been fine with the conversation taking place behind the safe confines of the ward.

"It's fine," I whispered, but her doubtful expression didn't change.

Once I broke the ward by stepping over the threshold, Ileana brushed past me.

"This is Dominic's doing?" she asked.

I nodded. "Dominic's magic is increasingly impressive," she said, pride replacing the irritation in her voice. She took in my apartment with a sweeping look before turning her appraisal to Emoni. A smile curled her lips. It was warmer than I remembered her extending to either me or Dominic.

In a warm and melodious voice, she said, "I'm here to help, not harm."

It made me wary of the ease with which she slipped into the facade of being innocuous.

"Is Helena alright?" she asked.

If she didn't know, I didn't feel comfortable telling her. She searched my face for something.

"Why did you ask that?" Was it intuition or a magical connection?

"She tried to come to me. Sabin reported seeing an apparition of her. She hasn't reappeared. I suspect her magic is being restricted because she was unable to speak. And because Dominic has you secured behind this ward, he's protecting you. What happened?"

Her concern made me push aside the fact that she was often the one who provided counterproductive suggestions, such as letting chaos ensue, killing a bunch of people, or causing a catastrophe and seeing who survived.

Emoni went to the kitchen and returned with a glass of water that she handed to Ileana. Taking a small drink from it, Ileana returned her attention to me. "She is in trouble?"

I nodded. "They're looking for her now."

She narrowed her gaze on me. "Who is looking for her?"

"Everyone available." I considered embellishing that finding her was top priority. It was top priority for Dominic, Anand, and Areleus. I wasn't convinced that Helena's return was at all important to any of the others. I doubted they cared about protecting the realms of the Underworld and the beings who dwelled there.

"Take me to the place she was taken from," Ileana demanded, placing the water on the table and leaving the apartment without awaiting a response.

When we didn't follow, she turned, piercing me with her icy glare. A shiver of fear ran through me, but it wasn't greater than my desire to avoid returning to the site of the violence, the people who saw me as a problem, and where I had nearly been abducted also.

I couldn't shake the discomfort of the Dark Caster's loss of interest in me once she had her sights on Helena. Finding Helena had to outweigh my fear.

I nodded. Emoni cuffed my arm, giving me a look that told me she wasn't going to leave me alone.

Ileana scowled her disapproval. "I am responsible for two lives," she complained.

At least she'd accepted our safety as her responsibility, albeit reluctantly. It was still some protection. I'd take it any way I could get it, although my confidence in the lengths she'd go to honor it was questionable. Before heading out, I marched over to Emoni's arsenal and grabbed the pepper spray I'd seen. Emoni grinned and revealed a stun gun. My friend wasn't the vigilante of justice she wanted to be, but at least she was prepared.

Emoni offered to drive. My preference would have been to borrow the car and leave her behind, but the look she cast in my direction discouraged any such suggestion.

Ileana sneered at Dominic's vehicle at the warehouse, as well as at the occupants. I'd assumed they would have left if they'd declined to join the search, because they remained targets if the Dark Caster returned. If Dominic was there, so were Areleus and Anand. Speculation ran rampant through my mind about what could have happened in the past few hours. Had they searched and failed? Had there been another attack before they could look for Helena? Had Areleus's inability to show any form of humility caused an eruption of violence rather than offers of assistance? Not knowing bothered me, but I remained steadfast next to Ileana while she examined the building and the property next to it and did a cursory scan before she made rote movements while making her way around the building and surrounding areas.

Lingering illuminations of gold and amber from her magic whirled in the air and faded. It would have been a beautiful spectacle if I didn't know that one was more than likely a compulsion spell to prevent anyone coming near the area, and I had no idea what the second one was. But the effortless way she laid down sigils and markings was similar to what she had done when she wanted to subdue someone she needed to question, which made me confident that she would be entering a building without the threat of magic being used against her.

Emoni and I trailed behind her while I explained to Emoni my hypothesis of what I suspected had just occurred. She stopped short of the entrance. "And you're okay with this?"

"How could I stop her? No, I'm not okay with any of the things going on. I've been dragged into this, and my only goal is to limit the harm to humans and the others. At this point we just have defensive measures."

"Defensive measures against a woman who can create creatures, block magic, and who has a propensity for violence as her first tactic," she grumbled. I pressed a finger to my lips, hoping she'd soften her voice as it was rising with each item she listed.

She nodded, ushering away fear and apprehension from her expression. "We're going to be okay," she whispered. Squaring her shoulders to stand taller, she displayed a bravado that her panting breaths betrayed. And her confidence disappeared completely when we were confronted with a group of shifters who had reverted to their human form. *Their naked human form.* With magic suspended, the witches couldn't clothe them.

The naked shifters pinned Ileana with malicious sneers. With immunity to magic, they wore the shock of it being used against them with anger. I suspected Ileana's link to animals played a part in that ability, but I wondered what her limitations were. They'd hate her for her power in the same manner they despised the royals.

Her appearance didn't spark recognition in any of the faces in the room. She quickly found Dominic among the sea of people and fixed a cutting look in his direction. He returned it, before shifting a glare in my direction. Tension and anger bracketed his frown before it quickly fell away along with his attention that he redirected to Ileana.

"I have one question," she said without an introduction or waiting for the commotion to die down from her magic-blocking spell. All eyes turned to her, commanding the room as she did with her unique presence that clearly wasn't of this world. "Why hasn't Helena been found?" she asked in a tone steeped with accusation.

"Mother, you've joined us." Dominic's attempt at diplomacy and to distinguish her as an ally not to be feared was lost on the group. She was a royal. A menacing entity with the ability to block their magic. An obvious threat. Ileana would never be considered an ally. And clearly had become an addition to the mounting problems.

I followed Ileana's eyes as they glided across the space, taking in the aftermath of a brutal skirmish, the energy still present in the room and the reddish-brown stains that had sunk into the pores of the concrete floor.

"We're discussing a strategy," Dominic offered. It might have been his desire to do so, but the unyielding looks of defiance contradicted his statement.

Emoni forced her gaze to stay away from the stains in the concrete. The putrid and undeniable smell of sweat, fear, and aggression lingered. The air was oppressive with potential and past danger and dread. All her efforts to ignore it failed. As did mine.

"We must be in full agreement of a truce," Dominic said. I couldn't figure out what had occurred that would lead Dominic to believe he couldn't trust the others. Although there would be limited trust when it was riddled with self-interest, the threat of betrayal, and tenuous loyalty because of a magical contract that they would surely circumvent if given the chance.

The set jaws and reluctant nods indicated the agreement was made under duress.

"If you aren't confident in this agreement, I will find my sister. And *only* find her. The shades and the Dark Caster and her acolytes will be your problem. May your survival be in your favor." If the last few hours had been spent negotiating with the group for their help, I could imagine Dominic was at the end of his patience. Areleus's fist balled at his side indicated that he was restraining himself from responding in the way he did best: violently. His reluctant display of diplomacy pulled his face into a baleful grimace.

Piecing together bits of the murmurs I could make out, body language, and expressions, it seemed Dominic had to form a rescue party but also quell the dissension in the group. If Helena could be abducted, confidence in the royals had diminished. Were they arrogant or foolish enough to believe they'd have a chance? The losses they'd suffered would have been exceptional, if not cutting down their numbers so severely they wouldn't stand a chance in hell of doing anything other than submitting. But unearned confidence often accompanied arrogance, and supernaturals had shown to have a disadvantageous amount of both.

"Just because we aren't happy about this truce and have grievances with Helena doesn't mean we don't understand the significance," Madeline provided. "If the Underworld is destroyed, the prisoners will be released, and I am not confident of our survival if Celeste isn't in the Perils." Her patronizing sneer vanished and was replaced by something I'd never seen on her. Gratitude? Humility? Or a mélange of both. "Thank you for returning Celeste to the Perils and preventing *your sister* killing her."

They had every right not to be enthusiastic about looking for someone who was so cavalier about sentencing them to certain death.

Dominic must have returned Celeste to her prison, which was why Helena, rather than Dominic, was there to offer me help. I wondered if the results would be the same if he hadn't been the one to return Celeste. Would we be looking for Dominic instead of Helena?

"We are one collective," added Emory, shamelessly unabashed by his current state of nudity situation. Then he looked at his cohorts. "The infighting left us vulnerable. We can't allow this to continue. We must be aligned, without limitations." There seemed to be a general acceptance of that. I was positive that the collective would be against the royals and their involvement, and was only agreeable to the truce because it was mutually beneficial.

"Why is he naked?" Emoni whispered, but with their hearing, the shifters and vampires heard her.

Before I could answer, Emory padded closer, smirking, locking his gaze with her. Emoni wasn't a stranger to a lot of attention from a wide assortment of men: you-don't-have-a-chance-in-hell; you're pretty, I'm pretty, let's date; I'm rich, that has to get me some points. But a naked dhole shifter with a villainous English accent had to be a first.

"It appears we don't have magic. So, we were forced back into our human form, and the ability for the witches to clothe us was taken as well." He directed a shrewd glare to Ileana.

"What type of shifter are you?" Unbothered by the nude Bond Villain, Emoni's interest remained piqued.

"Dhole," he said.

Fear and disgust was discarded like litter; excitement blazed in Emoni's eyes, smothering any display of apprehension. *My friend is weird.* It was a reluctant acceptance.

"And you can shift?" Because Anand was a non-shifting shifter, she hadn't been able to see a shift.

All eyes turned to Ileana, who nodded. It was doubtful the shifters cared about the dhole shifting to assuage my friend's curiosity. They wanted their ability to perform magic. People who possessed such power didn't like it restricted in any way. That had been made apparent to me by Helena's reaction when she attempted to stab her brother with a broken wine bottle when he performed a spell to block her magic. Along with the royals' gifts seemed to be an innate compulsion to do whatever was needed to obtain more power and abilities.

Moments after Ileana stepped out, the shifters' bodies contracted and shuddered as if fighting off a surge of magic that would force them back into their animal form. The dhole gave in to the magic and shifted, looking predatory as he padded around Emoni. Fascination had robbed my friend of all her self-protective instincts, and she knelt, positioning her face close to his but not before me giving her a reminder that dholes were aggressive predators. Him sharing a body with a human didn't change that. Ignoring my warning, Emoni had clearly decided that the predatory dhole was as harmless as a cute toy poodle and was treating him as such.

Please don't bite my friend.

"That one is human. How will that be handled?"

Emoni was too busy sinking her fingers into the fur of the predatory dog, so she missed the fact she'd become the subject of discussion.

A vampire stepped forward to handle the situation with compulsion. Emoni looked up from the animal and noticed that all eyes had turned to her and that a vampire with exposed fangs was just inches from her.

Blocked by Dominic, he revealed his fangs in warning, pulling a dismissive smirk from Dominic.

"She's fine. Your anonymity will remain. Luna is human

and knows."

From their looks, grumbles, and murmurs, I'd graduated from "his human" to something else. In that vicarious state between not quite human or supernatural. A place that garnered me more contempt than value.

The sharp hiss rang in the room before the vampire lunged at Emoni. Dominic caught him by the throat before tossing him to the other side of the room. Emoni sucked in a breath, shuffled back several feet, and Anand grabbed hold of her, pulling her to him. She nestled closer, a flare of fear in her eyes. Emoni fisted his shirt, burrowing closer to him. I wanted her to be cautious but not hammered by the reality of how easily her life could be snuffed. Anger placed an unbearable tightness in my chest and a thirst for revenge that felt bitter. I hated it.

"Stop," Dominic commanded Emory who, during the commotion, had shifted to human form. Slowly approaching Emoni, Emory seemed unsettled by her loss of interest, which he had clearly enjoyed. Her face was a sheet of fear and apprehension. Ragged breaths escaped and her tense stance made it clear she wanted to be anywhere other than in a room of the magically inclined.

Emory continued moving toward Emoni and Anand, but when she reared back farther into Anand he stopped and looked in the direction of the witches. With a casual wave from one of them, he was clothed.

He slowed his approach. His voice dropped to a low satin tone. Gentle and comforting. "Are you okay?" She barely bent her head into the nod.

"Lovely. Know that we aren't all like that. Your safety is a concern to us all. His behavior was unwarranted and deserving of Dominic's harsh response." He was slathering it on a little too thick and disingenuous.

From my short time with vampires, I'd noticed that they tended to be brusque, impulsive, and with a propensity for violence when protecting their anonymity and themselves. Emory's PR scrubbing of the vampire's misdeeds earned him a side-eye glare. He saw it, ignored it, but halted his advance toward her.

It had nothing to do with my look of disapproval and Anand's thunderstorm look that added to the tension in the room.

"It's fine. I understand you don't want people to know about you all, but is murder really necessary?" Emoni asked.

His brows drawn together, he looked back at the vampire who'd recovered and was avoiding Anand's challenging gaze that seemed like he was encouraging him to consider another attempt. "He wouldn't have killed you. The miscreant was going to compel you to forget." There was an effort to sound confident, but I wasn't buying it. Compelling someone took time.

"Messing with my mind?" she asked. Repulsion and anger overshadowed the fear.

He nodded. Disgust, anger, and disbelief competed for expression on her face. Guilt welled in me because I'd allowed Dominic to manipulate her memories after she'd been attacked with a *necri* spell. Although it was done to protect her, I still agreed with her. Manipulation of a person's world took away their autonomy and was a violation.

"We are done here. Finding my sister is the priority."

"I question your tactics. Should your sister be a priority since Areleus is handling that?" Ileana's emotion regarding Areleus's mission showed in her furrowed eyebrows, the flare of her nostrils, and the deep-seated scowl. She made no effort to hide it. Storm clouds homed in on Dominic.

A perceptive Madeline took note of it. "I believe that apprehending those who have aligned with the Dark Caster should take precedence over our efforts at finding Helena. It's not just the newly acquired magic that the Dark Caster possesses, we must also contend with shades that have weaponized against us. How can we be any help to you when we have those serious concerns?"

"I agree. I will handle the shades," Ileana offered returning to the room, commanding everyone's attention. "*Only* after Helena is found. I'm not sure if the Caster has discovered a way to gain access to her magic. You do not want to contend with anyone who possesses our magic *and* the Dark Caster's. None of us do." She smiled, a disarmingly genuine one. "I give you my word, the shades will no longer be an issue. We find Helena, we find the Dark Caster. I assure you she will not be a worry any longer, either."

Her oath accompanied a confidence that made everyone quickly agreeable. They wanted it over by any means, and Ileana was giving them what they wanted: clear destruction and an end to their problems.

"And the Awakeners that chose the opponents' side? What will happen to them?" asked a man in a small voice. I recognized him from the group of shamed Awakeners who had become allies. His carefully worded question was an indicator that he didn't want them dead. Once the dust had settled and the immediate threat gone, there was room for them to reconvene to complete their goals.

Several eyes moved to Ileana, who had her attention firmly on Dominic. Her lips were pressed into rigid lines, suppressing what I'm sure was a direct and unhelpful response that they'd be destroyed with the rest. That seemed to be her preferred tactic. Sensing that it might not achieve the diplomacy Dominic was aiming for, she kept it to herself.

"They will be captured," Dominic offered. "Handled in the manner that you wish."

It was apparently a mutually agreed upon action and without pushback. Directives were given on where to search, and everyone broke into smaller groups.

The royals and Anand stayed together.

10

Uncertainty lingered in the space after everyone had gone, but Dominic remained intently focused on me. His jaw clenched from holding back words that needed to be said. Blowing out a breath, Dominic's hand cuffed around my wrist as he led me out of the room.

Out of the sight and earshot of the others, he spun me around, pressing me into the wall. Fire blazed in his eyes; his face strained at his attempt to rein in his emotions. He closed his eyes, his breath sharpening. After several moments of tense silence, his eyes opened. They were simmering with unidentifiable emotions. He sank his fingers into my hair, guided my head up to rest his forehead against mine.

"Why are you here?" he asked in a strained voice.

"What?"

"Luna, you were safe behind a ward. Why did you break it and come here putting yourself in danger?"

"Ileana showed up looking for Helena. Did you expect me to tell her that Helena was missing and just give her directions to this place," I challenged. Seeing the warring emotions of relief, frustration, and anger, I attempted to temper my words, but it was difficult. His expectation that my safety took priority over everything was unrealistic and put me in a position of ignoring what was right.

"Yes. Never underestimate her. She wouldn't have had great difficulty finding this place."

"Exactly, I don't estimate your mother. I felt just as safe with her as I would be with you. Helena's missing, how can I just send her off with some vague directions to this warehouse?" My hands glided lightly over his arms until they came in contact with his hand and held it.

"Don't ask me to hide when I can help. Ileana needed my help." I whispered. "*And,* have you met her?" I teased. "She's not one you deny. Ileana was likely to level my apartment if I'd declined."

He cut his eyes as if it was absurd but didn't refute it. Because it was doubtful he could with certainty.

"I'm not asking you to do that. But I'm asking you to behave as someone who doesn't have magic, is considered by some as dangerous and the reason for all of this, and someone who can be used as a weapon against me," he admitted.

"I'm not being careless. If I thought for one moment I would compromise the situation or have been in danger, I'd have figured out another way."

"I know," he conceded. "It's…" The words were lost into the deep kiss he gave me, conveying his feelings in a way I doubt he could express in words.

Magic and warmth wrapped around me when he ended the kiss, sinking into me. "Luna," he said with reverence and slivers of frustration at finding himself in a place I doubt he'd ever been before.

"Helena," I said.

The mention of her name had him shrugging off the weight of the emotions and refocusing on the various problems that needed to be addressed.

After planting another soft kiss to my lips, forehead, and

cheek, he returned to the room with me close behind him. I gave Emoni a reassuring smile that did nothing to quell her inquiring look and the heated glare she shot in Dominic's direction. Her mounting fears and frustrations from the turmoil needed a target and he was it.

After a stifling quiet while everyone surveyed the room, Areleus said cryptically, "I need to check a place." He vanished before anyone could ask any questions.

"He's probably going to where he'd met Peter—" Dominic left out the day Helena and Areleus sided with Peter against Dominic in hopes of acquiring more power.

Both Dominic and Ileana gave the vacant space a look of suspicion. She frowned. "Be mindful of Areleus. His loyalties are tenuous when acquisition of power is on the line. You've never showed those flaws but"—her eyes softened as she looked at him—"your relationship with Helena has been riddled with misunderstanding."

Ileana had diplomatically placed a creative PR spin on her daughter trying to claw her brother on more than one occasion, and betraying him. She moved directly in front of him, concern blooming over her features, eyes whetted with curiosity.

"Helena's return is important to you?"

"I care for her safety." The strain of his conflicting emotions clung to his words, making his assertions sound insincere. "If her life is ever put in jeopardy, it needs to be because of betraying me, not being a pawn for power or destruction. I will not allow her magic to be used against us in any way."

Ileana's movements were graceful and light as she paced a small trail in the room, periodically sweeping her gaze around at the signs of the fighting. "If you were in the Dark Caster's position, tell me the ways you'd attempt to use Helena's magic," she said.

While Dominic considered her question, she watched

him with intense fascination and something that wavered between pride and apprehension.

"I'd use something similar to the Garon." he said. "*But,* use of it against Peter was only possible because the magic was the same. That is why it was used against Luna. I'm not aware of anything that could strip us of our magic. Even if such an object existed, would the Caster have the power to do it? "

"The Dark Caster didn't use anything to take my magic. It's not an ability Peter possesses, because when I denied him, surely he would have taken mine to increase his power," I said.

Ileana and Dominic considered this.

"You restricted Helena's magic. Can the same be done to the Caster?" Anand asked.

Dominic shook his head. "Her magic mirrors mine, which was how the sigils were created to restrict hers."

"Is magic mimicry possible?" Emoni asked, lifting her gaze from the floor where it had been directed while she listened to the discussion.

Ileana and Dominic froze at the idea. Perhaps with just standard magic it wasn't possible. Three times the magic, and Helena, changed the potential. The implication marred their faces with worry. Dominic's lips parted to speak before he gave his words more consideration.

"I don't know." The words slipped out in a low, stiff rumble, washing a look of concern onto Ileana's face. They'd never experienced powerlessness and weren't faring well at the idea.

"I need to speak with Peter again. There has to be a way for us to locate the Caster through him," Dominic said, exiting the warehouse and waving me to come with him. Emoni rushed to my side.

"If they can't be of help they are a hindrance," Ileana said when Dominic didn't stop Emoni, who'd somehow become my self-appointed guardian.

He spoke up. "Having a team is advantageous. It's the reason the Dark Caster went after Luna initially. With Luna's refusal, I suspect she'll take Peter as a consolation. I need to be there when that proposal is made. Make no mistake, Luna is still wanted. I want her at my side so she won't be taken."

Ileana's attention fixed on Emoni who met her look in a challenge, wearing her defiance like armor. "I won't let anything happen to my friend," Emoni asserted.

"Is there something you can do to prevent it?" Ileana responded with a taunting dark humor. It reflected her low opinion of the magicless.

Emoni ignored the question and headed out the door.

"They both will be protected," Anand added, closing the distance between him and Emoni.

As we neared the SUV, Dominic looked over his shoulder at his mother. "If I need anything, I will call on you. I will return Helena to you, where I think she should stay."

Ileana's jaw clenched, but I couldn't tell if it was because of Dominic's unsubtle way of asking her to leave or that she'd no longer be welcomed in his world. I clung to what that meant: When this was over, Dominic planned to be Lord of the Underworld and his father no longer a situation.

Ileana's disapproving gaze was felt with every step until we were in the vehicle. Emoni remained stiff alongside us. Even her breaths seemed to have changed to infrequent and shallow in an attempt to remain inconspicuous.

A look of shocked wariness was shared between me and Emoni when there was no mention of taking us home and we headed in the direction of Peter's apartment.

Why did they want us with them? Was it safer to be around them than at home? Was our presence necessary for the best outcome? I was sure of only one of the three things: that if the goal was the least amount of violence, death, and human autonomy, our presence was necessary. Maybe that was our role in this. Who knew?

———

Dominic's persistent knocks at Peter's went unanswered. The knocks were a simple courtesy. A small whirl of his fingers near the door, and it opened for us. Expecting to see a bedraggled Peter, I was surprised by the empty apartment and all evidence of his failed magic gone.

Dominic and Anand searched, looking for reasons for his departure and hints to where he'd gone.

I looked for the book he'd used to communicate with the Dark Caster. It was gone also. Had Peter finally had success with his attempts to communicate with Ophelia, or, after I refused her, was he chosen as an alternate? Despite all evidence that the book was gone along with Peter, I continued scanning the room for it.

My eyes snagged on an ivory-color infinity knot at the far end of the room. Moving closer to it, I felt ominous energy suffusing from it, crawling over my arm, making it tingle. Tendrils of the strange magic lingered. When it settled, I was tugged forward. I dug my heels in, but it didn't help. The pull was too strong, and I found myself just inches from the object. I winced at the sharp blaze of heat that wrapped around the skin just above my wrist. I pulled my attention from the magical object to the red symbol that appeared on my wrist. It was identical to the black one that suddenly appeared on the infinity knot.

Just a few inches from it, I grappled with the over-whelming urge to touch it. *Don't touch it*, I commanded myself. But the demands of the enigmatic tool were too great.

"Luna," Emoni's concerned voice resonated in my mind, which was becoming increasingly fuzzy. *Don't touch it.*

But it was demanding to be touched, held. Used.

I knew I shouldn't and contracted my muscles to force resistance against the strong magical pull. Before I could reach for it, Dominic was at my side, pulling me away. Positioned in front of me, his body became a wall, preventing me nearing it.

It didn't stop the need. And when he picked up the object, Emoni grabbed my arm and jerked me to her before I could touch it. She kept a firm hold on me.

"Luna," she said. I didn't respond. She cupped my face and searched it for information. I wanted to speak, but words just didn't come freely. They felt locked. There was only one goal: Touch the ivory knot.

"What is this?" She lifted my arm to inspect the mark. It throbbed and felt warm. Her urgency made her touch rougher than I'm sure she intended. Her nails digging into my skin was enough of a jolt of pain to clear my head a little. My thoughts were split between listening to my friend and my curiosity about the object. Desire to answer her question and to hold the magical tool.

Dominic growled out an angry spew of curses. Walking around us, he stopped spewing long enough to whisper an invocation. Similar sigils that he'd used to restrict his sister and a witch's magic during a fight formed a circle around us. The enigmatic pull of the magic stopped, my head cleared, and the need to grab the object stopped. I was unable to explain what had happened or make sense of it because my attention was drawn to Emoni's series of questions.

"Why is she marked? What did you do? Why is this happening to us?" Followed by a promise of bodily harm, removal of their magic, teaching them true fear, and an impressive list of threats she didn't have the physical strength to perform, wasn't anatomically able to perform, and without magic and preternatural speed or strength could never perform.

"How are you, without any magic, planning to destroy all magic?" I asked in response to one of the more unreasonable threats. Her smirk mirrored mine, and the tight grip she had on my arm loosened, but her attention stayed on the symbol.

"I don't have a plan, but anger makes a lot of things possible," she snapped with a laugh at her own ridiculous response. I needed her calm, because anger from Dominic and Anand was rampaging through the room.

With the infinity knot in his hand, fire blazed from Dominic's other hand.

"Do not destroy it!" Areleus commanded in a surly voice, a quick slice of his finger in the air extinguishing the fire. "Not yet," he tacked on at the challenge in Dominic's expression that overtook his look of surprise at his presence.

"What happened?" Areleus asked me.

"Magic touched me. Lured?" I said, my explanation lacking a surety they all wanted. It was an alluring pull of magic, but nothing like Dominic's, which teased and seduced me. Instead, it was a command to be obeyed.

"Magic pulled me to it." With more confidence, I told them about the flare of heat, the symbol forming on my arm that remained, and the urge I felt to touch the object.

"They want her!" Areleus said. "If she had touched it, I suspect a spell similar to the *temporalibus* would have put someone in her place."

"Not possible without something of hers: hair, blood, intimate clothing," Dominic said.

"Or phone." I was positive I'd left it at Peter's, or during my last visit. Could anything of mine have been used?

"Perhaps they know of a spell that wouldn't require those things," Dominic speculated.

"It would have switched me with Peter?" I asked. Had he been abducted or had he left willingly? Was he being used as a pawn again?

"I doubt it. Probably with someone inconsequential. An

unknowing or unwilling participant." A person minding their own business and swooshed into an unknown apartment. I hated the feeling when the *temporalibus was used and I'd found myself swept away and in the Perils prison where Peter had been housed.*

"Ophelia—that's the name she gave me. And she does consider Peter inconsequential."

Dominic shook his head, frowning at the ward that enclosed me. "Probably not now. He's an asset who likely has had his magic returned. There is power in numbers, which is why they want you. Three people with their magic would be formidable."

"Why?" Emoni blurted. "She lacks the very thing you all seem to have too much of, a thirst for power and violence. She'd be no help to anyone."

It was probably the first time that being useless was an attribute.

"I'm sure there'd be a line of people willing to possess that magic. I don't understand why it has to be her." Emoni's voice broke at the end with a desperation of a seemingly hopeless situation. I was starting to feel it, too.

"Because she's able to carry the magic. It's her magic," Areleus said, keen eyes on me. He stepped toward me, eying the ward that surrounded me and Emoni, but was quickly blocked by Dominic before he could further close the distance.

A cynical smile curled Areleus's lips. "*And* because Luna possesses the one thing that the other Casters do not. Immunity. Whether she burns down the world, puts us or others in danger, or becomes a complete menace, my son will not hurt her."

I'd never heard acknowledging a link sound so tyrannically cruel.

Despite having Dominic as a barrier and being enclosed in a ward that I wasn't sure Areleus could break, I took as many steps back from him as I could while remaining in the circle.

Areleus's eyes jumped to the infinity knot in Dominic's hand.

"Keep it intact. It may be of some use," he urged.

"Why are you here?" Dominic asked.

"I figured you'd be here. Without the use of location spells, how can we find Helena? Why isn't she putting effort into helping us? Helena is tenacious, so how is she being held so easily?" Areleus said the last part in a whisper, posing the question to himself.

"Her magic has been compromised. She attempted to escape to the Vita, but it was unsuccessful," I reminded him. Something that Ileana had told him, but anger had made him distracted.

Areleus's eyes darkened. After exhaling a ragged breath, he said, "They can't restrict her magic. No one can."

"It has happened. We are dealing with a Caster who's managed to elude being caught and has learned how to steal magic from other Casters without the assistance of a magical object. Simply using a spell. She shouldn't be underestimated."

Areleus's covetous thirst for more power sparked in his eyes. His loyalty couldn't be trusted, and I wouldn't put it past him to cozy up to the Dark Caster as a way to grab it.

Dominic fixed his father with an assessing look. I suspected he thought the same. The exchange of hostility was undeniable with the knowledge that at the end, one of them probably wouldn't survive. Observing the tension, Emoni gave my hand a squeeze.

"How do we remove the mark from Luna?" Her intentions were obvious in the sharp look she shot them. She wanted the mark removed and us as far away from this situation as possible.

Areleus relaxed his stance but kept an attentive eye on Dominic, who remained a wall between me and Areleus.

Ignoring Emoni's question, Areleus directed his response to Dominic. "Use Luna to find Helena. They want her." He glanced at the spelled infinity knot. He side-stepped Dominic to get closer to me, triggering an immediate reaction from Dominic who pushed him back several feet. A reaction that seemed to be out of instinct, not malice. Areleus's exposed claws were a declaration of violence.

"Do you believe for one moment she will be safe? They want her and will have her. Should we fall and our realms be destroyed for her? You've lost sight of your responsibility. You've listed all Ophelia's abilities and yet you don't see a need to impede any further acquisition of power? With her having the use of Helena, you will be at a severe disadvantage. Are you willing to accept that for a woman?"

"A woman I love."

My mouth parted at the confession that came from him so freely and the raw vulnerability on his face. Areleus's claws retracted and the anger washed from his face. The atmosphere was charged with unspoken emotions. Dominic positioned himself defensively, ready to shield and safeguard me from any harm from Areleus.

Dominic's father's face grew mild as he adopted the persona of a person who valued love, but his emotions were clouded by his desperate need for his daughter to be returned. The act was convincing, but I knew what lurked behind the amiable expression.

"Then creating a situation where she's not in danger should be important to you. They want her and won't stop until they have her. You've always been pragmatic, but that ability seems to have escaped you. Allow Luna's connection to be a way to obtain proximity to them and end this. You have the means. I know you do."

I wasn't wholly convinced that Peter was with Ophelia,

because I recalled the venom in her words when she spoke of him. I couldn't imagine a willingness to return his magic and work with him. But neither could I imagine wanting to destroy the race of vampires, subjugate witches, and make shifters vulnerable to magic to garner power over them. I didn't have great insight into people who were willing to do such things. Peter was skilled and with the same aligned interest and a mutual hate for the royals. That would be advantageous to her.

I was out of my league. I wanted out of this situation as well. Dominic's confession stayed in the forefront of my mind. He loved me and he was part of this situation. With all the surging feelings and the turbulent situation, Dominic was a surety and constant. I wanted him. I was still sorting out whether it was love.

"Areleus is right," I admitted. *Ugh, that didn't feel good at all.* Agreeing with him left a bitter taste. "If I can be used to locate them, then I'll agree to it."

The heat of Emoni's shocked gaze bored into me. Ignoring it led to her nails piercing the hand she'd kept a hold on.

Turning to face me with an expression that settled between awe and confusion, Dominic offered me a grim smile. "Your bravery always exceeds my expectations."

At face value it looked like bravery. Bad actions and decisions often disguised themselves that way. I was making the best decision that would allow Helena to be found, stop the Dark Casters, maintain the integrity of the Underworld, and continue my relationship with Dominic without the chaos of the supernatural world.

Am I asking too much? Probably.

Dominic handed the bespelled infinity knot to Anand. "Will you take this far from us, please?" In the small apartment, Anand moved away and into a room that I suspected was the bedroom.

Dominic disengaged the ward. "How do you feel?" he asked.

"Fine."

He positioned himself directly in front of me. "Release her hand," he instructed Emoni. Several seconds later, she released it.

Everyone kept a keen eye on me like they were expecting me to bolt toward the object. I was half expecting it, too. But I didn't feel that enigmatic pull or any tendrils of magic pricking at my skin. Nothing.

I shook my head.

Dominic whispered, "Come closer." He was looking past me, addressing Anand. An extensive amount of time was dedicated to determining the distance I needed to be from the object to prevent it eliciting a response.

Though the distance seemed to be about six feet, Dominic was overly cautious, asking Anand to take it home to his wing of the house. "We'll be there soon."

"Why?" Anand asked, keeping himself and the bespelled object a safe distance from me.

"I need the Book of Umbra."

The mention of the dangerous book that Dominic kept from his father for fear of abuse piqued Areleus's attention. Anand and Dominic took notice.

"Should I escort her home?" Anand asked Dominic, gesturing at Emoni.

She wasn't having it. Shoring up for an argument and protest, she locked her arm through mine.

"It's okay," I whispered, trying to disengage from the hold.

"What exactly are you okay with, Luna? Me not hearing from you for days? Me wondering if things were successful? Or being forced to pretend things were normal while wondering if I'd ever see you again?"

The sad desperation in her voice compounded my remaining guilt. Dominic studied my face then moved to

Emoni's. I'd accepted that the royals weren't moved by human emotions and the decisive look on his face supported it. It wavered when his gaze returned to me. Everything would be done to keep her safe, and I wanted her with me.

He nodded. Placing me in front of him, he held me tight and kept a loose grasp on Emoni. "Close your eyes," he instructed her, and when they opened, we were at the door of his home.

Emoni stepped back, holding her head, trying to regain composure after the unsettling travel that left a person off-kilter. It wasn't dizziness but an airy feeling of losing your bearings.

Immediately and without a word, Areleus entered the house.

11

  moni stopped and looked around at the bleakness of their world without any hints of the midday sun that we'd left. After taking in the exterior of the castle-like stone building, her brows inched together at the dark grays and deep currants, the bushes encircling the building and the lush forests next to it.

Losing step with me as we entered the home, her head snapped in the direction of the departing guards who followed Areleus. Slowly she took in the grandeur of the room. Her appreciation for art extended beyond music, and it showed as she moved throughout the area to look at the art and sculptures atop pedestals. A smirk curled at her lips at the number of winged sculptures, I was confident finding the same irony that I had. At least her first visit was as a guest; mine had felt more like imprisonment.

"It's beautiful, isn't it," I said, moving close to her, aware of Dominic's watchful eyes.

"I had great expectations." She looked over everything visible. "And it still has exceeded it. But the darkness is creepy."

"Wait till you see the garden and the black flowers," I told her with a grin. Expecting the information to pique her interest, I was surprised when it didn't. Instead, she returned a tight reserved smile, her eyes skating over me and moving to Dominic.

He looked between the two of us, surveyed the room as if he was trying to look at it through Emoni's eyes. Then his gaze returned to Emoni with intent focus. Expressionless, I couldn't figure out what went through his mind. He excused himself, and in the graceful sweep of preternatural movement, he was out of sight.

"What happens when things go further with Dominic? Will you stay here?" Emoni asked, seemingly having difficulty looking away from the space Dominic had occupied just seconds ago. It was a brazen reminder of how far from human he was.

My response was quick and reflexive before I could give it any consideration. I shook my head. I didn't want to live here or be part of this world. Not this part of it. I just wanted Dominic. Was it possible to have him and not all the things connected to him?

"Is he willing to give this up to be with you? Is that possible?"

I blinked back tears of frustration and answered with a half shrug. The words wouldn't form. There were many things in my mind that needed to be sorted out.

"If he can't, will you always be in some form of danger because of your relationship with him? Oh, come on," she scoffed in response to my look of confusion.

"Once this is over, the Dark Casters stopped, edicts in place and reinforced, infighting put to rest, and everyone confident I didn't have connections to the Dark Casters and their magic, I'd become a non-issue."

"You're being overly optimistic. Naïve. I may not know

much about their world, the politics, or the dysfunction that accompanies being a person with magic, but I can spot when people despise someone. No matter how this situation is managed, there is sheer animosity for Dominic and his family. And the looks they gave at the mere mention of Helena."

Helena hadn't made a positive impression on Emoni during their first meeting, either.

"Are you prepared to have a relationship with the Lord of the Underworld?"

"That's not his title."

"Not yet, but whenever he"—she scrunched her nose—"when they… when the… you know?" *When he kills his father.* It was a distasteful thing to think and even harder to say. I was surprised at her astute reading of the situation.

"I'm quite observant. One would have to be particularly dense not to see the malicious intent they have for each other. It will end badly for one of them. The hostility between them won't be resolved by something trite like a spirited game of chess. Just straight to murder." She winced.

"You gathered all of this from a day with them, yet you don't realize Gus is in love with you?" I asked in an attempt to pull her thoughts from the dark place they had clearly delved into.

"He's not."

Her selective observational skills should be studied.

Emoni's lips parted to say something else but closed, her teeth gripping her lips, leaving me speculating whether she could read my thoughts on my face. Dominic had confessed that he loved me, and we hadn't had a chance to discuss it. Before I could get into the subject with Emoni, I wanted to talk to him and make sense of my complex feelings. My heart wanted to throw caution to the wind, but my mind was in a perpetual state of risk analysis assessment.

Emoni studied me for a few minutes before allowing herself to be distracted by the sculptured art.

"What happened between you and Jackson can't factor into whatever decision you make." Jackson cheating with a former best friend had crossed my mind and the betrayal still stung. But Dominic and Jackson were entirely different and so was this situation.

"I hadn't really thought about it," I said.

She frowned and mouthed, "Liar."

"Okay, I did, a little." I brought my fingers closer together leaving an inch of space. She closed the distance between us and spaced my fingers wider.

"If it was that little, your face didn't know it. This family is a mess, magic is the absolute worst—I stand by that. I don't care that I find it a little fascinating, I miss my wonderful world of blissful ignorance. But with everything that's going on, your life in constant danger and dealing with the fucking Lord of the Underworld, there's still an ease to you that I haven't seen in a long time. You were never truly at ease with Jackson." She shrugged. "Could be him, or the fact you're getting laid," she tacked on, beaming.

"He's a prince," I corrected.

"I know what his title is. I'm getting used to his new position and designation."

"You don't even call him prince—"

"Not going to, or lord. I'm just making a point." The silence was heavy but the mirth that lingered in her was a welcome comfort. "I really don't want to be that person—but I have to be because I'm always going to look out for you. I know it's easier to think things will get better and resolve and you'll have your old life back, with the addition of a sexy man and all its perks"—she sighed, giving the home a once over—"but I think it'll be more of the same. Consider that with any decision you make and determine if it's worth it. If he's worth it. I think you already know that. I'm just the voice of reason you need to hear."

She wasn't wrong.

"Let me show you the library," I offered in a jarring topic switch. She was the voice of reason, but it needed to be delayed in place of more pressing things. Emoni wasn't likely to drop the subject without some other distraction, and their breathtaking library would be a worthy redirection.

I waved her forward, navigating through the home and ignoring Emoni's smirk.

"You've already made yourself at home."

Standing at the entrance of the library she exhaled a breath of appreciation. A slow rove of the full bookcases, the ladder that allowed access to the taller stacks, and the seating. The whimsical look dropped from her expression as she snapped her attention to her left, where she got a glimpse of Sabin.

"What the fuck?" she said under her breath, her undivided attention on him.

Mine was on Ileana who accompanied him. She'd arrived from another entrance, allowing direct access to Dominic's wing of the house to avoid Areleus being aware of her presence.

My interest overrode polite restraint. I quickly moved toward them with Emoni on my heels. We cleared a surprising amount of ground and were at the bottom of the stairs by the time they were midway. Sabin looked over his shoulder with a mysterious glitter in his eyes. He greeted me with a devilish smirk before offering one to Emoni. She stopped on the step and stared after him.

Sabin was enjoying her response until Ileana called him. He hurried up the steps, following her in the direction of Dominic's office.

Stricken, Emoni hadn't moved from the spot on the steps. Her lips slightly parted and her eyes sharpened, still looking at where Sabin had stood. "Was that the creepiest or the most exquisite thing I've ever seen?" she asked herself aloud.

"For me it's a little of both."

She'd known about Ileana's creatures from my recounting of my time in Vita, Ileana's realm, but hearing about the creatures and seeing them was quite different. By the time we were upstairs, I could tell from Emoni's flustered look that she hadn't resolved how she felt about Sabin.

They'd disappeared into a room. I headed toward Dominic's office where he met me in the hallway. The dim lights cast a soft glow, accentuating the intensity of his gaze. His eyes homed in on me, searching for information that was easily revealed.

He leaned down, whispering against my ear, "We should talk." The warmth of his breath against my ear, his lips brushing against it, and the commanding hold he had on my waist was firm but not overpowering, an odd comfort. I couldn't pull my eyes from his when they connected with mine again, stirring the spectrum of complex and intense feelings I hadn't resolved. The weight of his gaze bore down, and I saw hints of what I was experiencing mirrored in his eyes. He kept them on me as he spoke to Emoni. "To the left of the hallway, there is a sitting room with a balcony that overlooks the garden." It was his indirect way of asking her to leave. She got the hint and ignored it.

"Where's the panther?" she asked.

Dominic canted his head at the enigma that was my friend, who'd discarded any sense of self-preservation in lieu of satisfying her curiosity, and was exhibiting intrigue and wariness in her question.

"It is probably best to go to the sitting area," Anand urged in an uncompromising tone, having arrived with the stealth and silent grace that allowed him to be unnoticed until that moment.

Emoni and I startled at his sudden presence, but Dominic wasn't surprised.

Anand nudged his chin in the direction of the sitting room.

"I'd like to view the library and then the garden, since I'm being asked to leave," she countered. "And where's the prison?"

"We'll go to the library and garden." Anand changed course toward the stairs. "Not the prison. I've gathered that you are quite persistent. Let me assure you that you're not more than I am. We have our itinerary, and there won't be any deviations from it." His deep chuckle came in response to Emoni's sneer.

Dominic's fingers laced through mine as he guided me to his bedroom. Closing the door behind me, he led me to the sofa. Pulling me into his lap, he cradled me against his chest. "I should not have said that to anyone before I said it to you."

"It's fine." The public declaration was undoubtedly as shocking to him as it was to me.

"It's not fine for me. I wanted to tell you. Should have told you earlier in a more fitting moment than you behind a ward, afraid for your life and once again a tool in a situation not of your making. My father needed to understand the gravity of my feelings and that it drives the decisions I make and the actions I take. Your life and safety aren't up for compromise."

The warmth of his body and words was alluring, but I had a longing to see his face as he said them. Turning to face him, my legs astride, I ran my fingers over the pronounced angles of his jaw and the determined lines of them.

"Say it just to me," I asked softly.

The sharp intensity in his eyes gradually subsided, replaced by a gentle, tender expression that he reserved for me. The quiet longing was evident in his gaze, concealed behind an aura of danger, cool disposition, and casual arrogance that I'd observed during our first meeting.

Leaning into me, in a hushed murmur, he confessed.

"I love you."

It felt like a caress without any expectation of it being returned.

That's what urged the words to spill from me with ease.

"I love you, too."

It was the second time I'd ever declared my love to a man. I tried not to make the comparison of Jackson's pronouncement that came weeks after I'd said it to him. It wasn't a declaration of his affections of love but rather a surrender.

I adored Dominic's confession and wanted to hear it again. But before I could make that request, he drew me closer with gentle yet commanding touches. The power of magic crackled in the air and moved around me. I'd never untangle magic and Dominic's sensual touch as his hand slipped under my shirt, kneading at my skin, sending rushes of heat through me. The world and its problems momentarily faded into insignificance.

Our lips met in a gentle touch before escalating to a fervent storm. A kiss that spoke of all the emotions and things we hadn't explored. His lips were infused with fiery need and a craving I wanted to satisfy.

Our bodies melded together, him hardening under me. Heavy lidded when he pulled away, half-smiling at my soft pants, he murmured, "When will you move in with me?"

"What...why...what?" I stammered. The words doused me like a splash of cold water.

His chest rumbled from his laughter. "Is that a yes?"

"It's a what?" I shook my head.

He nuzzled against my neck, jaw, and against my hair, accentuating the touches with soft kisses and nips along my neck.

"Little Luna," he growled in a low husk.

He pulled away, resting back against the sofa. All humor and levity was gone from his face, a dark cast of concern in its place. "You're far more careful with your residence than your life. Why would you agree to be used as a lure for Ophelia?"

I knew that topic would resurface, accompanied by a lecture in some form.

"Because Areleus is right. Despite my intentions, Ophelia will want me, and hiding isn't an option. I want this over and —" I let the rest remain unspoken. He didn't need a reminder of how much I wanted out of their world because it would be impossible for him not to believe he was included in it.

"I'm part of this world." His fingers resumed rubbing the skin of my lower back, making me put a great deal of effort into staying focused. "It can't be separated, no matter how much you want it to be that way." He burst the delusional bubble I was clinging to.

"Have you tried?" I pressed. Why would he? Immediately I regretted the question although I was curious about the answer. The silence stretched without an attempt at a response. I took it as a tacit no.

When his lips parted to answer, I covered them with mine. A hard raw kiss that he quickly responded to. His fingers sank into my hair, pulling me into him. His tongue exploring my mouth with a primal lust, my body responding. Nipples becoming hard against him. The friction of our bodies pressed together, heightening the response. His hardness pressed against me. We pulled away, both of our eyes traveling to where we connected, aware that nothing could be done about it now. I shifted my weight and scooted back a little, which only served to make his arousal more obvious. He smirked.

"Helena, Peter, and Ophelia," I whispered, as if he could forget those issues.

A shadow crossed over his features, darkening his eyes.

They sharpened as they held mine. "I don't like the idea of using you as bait—"

"Incentive," I corrected with a half smile.

He wore the frustration heavily in his expression. "I found Dark Casters before and I could do it again."

"Both evaded being found by you, and Ophelia is more skilled than Peter." And, I suspected, ruthless. "It's not just subjugating the others you have to worry about, it's the fall of this realm. Or worse, whatever her plans are for it."

"And it's only a matter of time before she finds a way to use Helena," he added, "or Helena allows herself to be used with the promise of more power."

I'd considered that briefly but didn't want to bring that to the forefront and have it be a reminder that he couldn't wholly trust his sister. Surely it affected his motivation for finding her.

"It would have the best results and satisfactory outcome."

"With Peter and Ophelia dead."

Failing in my attempt at a neutral voice, sorrow and judgment seeped into it. "The way the Dark Casters were *handled* is why things are this way."

"It's this way because of how they are. You've heard their plans. Fully aware of the lengths they are willing to go through to achieve them. What options are there?"

"You've managed to restrict the others' magic and imprison them. I don't believe they should go unpunished, but does it have to be death?"

It was always death. Destruction and death. Perhaps I was more optimistic about them than any of their behavior warranted.

Amber eyes scoured over my face; his lips formed a pensive line. When his head canted to the side, it curled into a smile. "You believe this show of kindness would change things?" he asked, curiosity woven in every word. It made me recall him telling me how the long years of living had removed them further from their humanity. Dominic's piercing curious eyes turned softer. I served as a reminder of something that had diminished in him and his family.

"I don't think it would change things significantly, but with everything that has happened, I believe the slightest display of ki—" I nixed the use of "kindness" because for some odd reason they had an aversion to it. And "compassion." As if I was calling them insignificant and ensuring they would be perceived as pushovers. "Valuing lives other than yours and your family's will work in your favor. The Awakeners, they're just looking for a reason to dissent and start over again, no matter the promise of punishment."

He had to have seen their humbled looks of regret. They were a poorly organized group with grand ideas, without the power or the means to be successful in their plans. They weren't even cohesive enough to collectively agree or decline allying with the Dark Caster. I was certain if the same was posed by the Conventicle or the New Conventicle, they all would have been in or out. There wouldn't have been any defectors.

Dominic inhaled a breath. Exhaling it, he stood, holding me as he did. He eased me to my feet, then took my hand. "I love hearing your perspective, it comes from such a pure place," he said, traipsing toward the door, taking shorter steps to help me keep up.

"Is that the polite way of saying naïve?" I asked.

"No, I meant exactly what I said." Accustomed as he was to the options of killing everyone, letting destruction reign, cleaning up the mess, or sheer violence and subjugation, I was a different voice and less sought after alternative.

"I don't know if it's the most pragmatic way. Don't hold it against me if it isn't a consideration I can make," he said, stopping in the hallway midway to his office. "If you are to be a lure, then my sole objective is to ensure that you come back to me. I won't be gentle with lives if it is at the risk of yours."

How could I object to that? *Nah, sacrifice me to save people who'd let me die for a Starbucks gift card.*

I nodded. He turned and we continued toward his office. "I have a plan that will work. It is more dangerous than I'd like but the best option. I don't believe you will be in the most danger."

"Then who will be?"

"Me."

12

Me. Dominic's last words were playing on a loop in my head. He would be the one in danger? What plan would put him in danger? Would he sacrifice himself for his sister? Making our way toward his office, I tugged his hand. "Emoni," I whispered. With his life in jeopardy, I felt even more protective of my friend. Despite knowing she was safe with Anand, I felt an overwhelming urge to see her for myself.

Dominic changed course and we looked in the library but didn't find them. He ushered me to the kitchen where I'd first seen the garden with the peculiar exotic flowers of black roses, Black Forest calla lilies, and bat orchids.

"Anand," Dominic said, his voice raised slightly higher. It didn't take very long for Anand to appear, with a noticeably bewildered Emoni next to him. I knew it was in response to Anand answering Dominic's call that she couldn't hear. An ability that I continued to find unsettling despite the multiple times I'd witnessed it. It had to be the pinnacle of eeriness for her.

As she managed to work her way through the discomfort, I took in the batch of exotic flowers from the garden in her hand and then looked to Anand, wondering if my friend's curiosity had her pilfering flowers or if he'd given them to her.

"I couldn't leave without these," she admitted. Moving closer to me she whispered as if there wasn't any possibility of her being heard. "I haven't decided if it's creepy or alluring." It seemed to pertain to more than just the garden, but the Underworld and Anand as well.

"Will you come with me?" Dominic said to Anand. "Can you find your way to the library?" Dominic asked Emoni. "Or we can direct you to another room or the bedroom you'll be staying in so you can get acclimated to it," he added in response to her look of apprehension.

"Bedroom?" Her eyes snapped from Dominic to me, widening in panic.

"It won't be for longer than two days," he offered in clarification.

With her sharp intake of breath, I knew she was quickly succumbing to the fears and ominous thoughts that she'd managed to keep at bay. Overtaken by the feeling that leaving was no longer an option.

"If I wanted to leave now, could I?" she blurted, ignoring me grasping her hands in an effort to calm her.

"Despite it being unwise and unsafe, we'd let you leave," Anand responded quickly, her mounting unease unable to be ignored. After assessing his face for a long moment, she looked to Dominic. Clearly not used to making so many concessions to a human—which he had a difficult time hiding, his lips pulled into a pinched line—he confirmed with a barely noticeable nod.

Her rigid posture relaxed with her exhalation. "Bedroom, please." Anand placed his hand on her back, guiding her in the opposite direction of where we were going.

She stopped abruptly. "I need a vase for these," she said. "I don't want them to…" Her eyes were firmly fixed on me. "I want them to survive."

The restless tension inundated the space. "They will," Dominic said. Moving with slow, purposeful steps, he disappeared into one of the rooms and returned with a vase.

"Join us once she is settled," Dominic said to Anand. Despite not being offered any further information, Anand appeared to have an understanding of the situation.

"And where would that be?" Emoni asked.

A smirk slid over Dominic's lips, and his eyes narrowed on her. It was a look I'd seen him give too often to those he deemed to possess inconsequential power but still attempted to assert dominance over him.

I understood Emoni's grimace because his look held hints of contempt and condescension. "You are very special to my Luna. Understand that you've been extended an exceptional amount of grace. I will not stand for Luna to be harmed. Ever. There is no need to question my every move."

He started to back away but before he could turn to leave, she blurted, "It won't stop me worrying about her. If you can't even give me something as simple as her location, don't expect me to place my unwavering trust in you."

Her tremulous voice softened the edges of Dominic's dark smirk. "Office. She's going with me to the office." I grabbed his hand and squeezed it, urging him not to disclose the possibility of Sabin being there. Emoni's curiosity had proven to be a weakness. Guilt over what this situation had done to her made me reluctant to have her involved in the meeting.

His response seemed to be enough, and she allowed Anand to lead her away.

Reeling from Dominic disclosing that he'd be the sacrifice, I was hesitant to enter the office. Bringing my hand to his lips, he pressed a kiss to it before releasing it and entering the room. Sabin was perusing the collection of books on the shelf, and Ileana had taken a seat at the desk and was examining a weathered, leatherbound book with gilded pages and illuminated writing. The hum of magic could be felt from across the room.

"You've made yourself at home," Dominic said to her, a tick in his jaw.

"The presence of the Book of Umbra can't be denied. It was easy enough to find."

"For you."

It was obvious that the task wasn't easy for Areleus or even Helena. If they were able to detect the book, Dominic wouldn't be in possession of it. They would have taken it and dedicated an unreasonable amount of time and resources trying to discover a way to get it open.

Dominic examined the book. "You didn't try to leave with it?"

"Why would I, when you made it clear you needed it to find the Dark Casters and your sister?"

The clench in his jaw relaxed along with his expression. Constant betrayal from the ones he loved seemed to have planted a distrust of everyone in his family. He nodded.

"*And* if that was my desire," she said, allowing her finger to graze over the area near the book, prompting a bronze illuminating shell to cover it, "it would be impossible. But I was able to find it and bring it to the desk. However, I never tried to leave the room with it." Pride lit her eyes.

Dominic couldn't weave spells like witches could, but he had a gift for combining complementary spells that were just as effective. He'd explained it was more time consuming, although his proficiency with it didn't support that assertion. He'd mastered magic and he seemed to be more adept at wards and protection spells than anyone else in his family.

"You are the most deserving of ruling," she said, leaning

forward. Their warring intense gazes couldn't be held comfortably by anyone else. "Make it so."

"That might not be possible," he admitted.

A wave of incredulous shock rippled through her expression before settling into a deep-seated scowl of disappointment. Then she turned from him, sending an icy gaze in my direction, looking for answers that I couldn't provide.

"The Book of Umbra," Areleus breathed out in excitement as he swept past Anand at the front door and at lightning speed made his way toward the book. As quick as the strike of a snake, he grabbed for it. Rebounded by a thrust of force, his hand made several rote movements while he whispered a spell. It failed. After his second unsuccessful attempt, his blazing eyes snapped to Dominic.

"He's quite clever. Is the ward keyed to emotions?" Ileana asked. "Even the cloaking of it is different than anything I've seen before." She directed the question to Dominic.

"Yes, to emotions and specifically to him," he said, shooting Areleus a contentious look. "And now Helena," he tacked on. Ileana didn't react, accepting that Helena, like her father, couldn't be trusted.

It took a great deal of effort for Areleus to marshal all expressions from his face, although he still couldn't hide the disdain that shone in his eyes.

Ileana's cool chuckle broke the contemptuous silence, and I was grateful for it. Hostility thick and arrant in the air, I was concerned that they'd act on it and nothing would be accomplished.

The acquisition of power must be stronger than any drug, leaving those who yearned for it willing to do anything for it. It was clearer than ever in the nonverbal exchange between Ileana and Areleus. Had they ever even liked each other? From the appearance of things, it was the union of two people with a clear purpose. One that they achieved. They had two extremely powerful children who possessed the ability to be pitiless and violent when needed.

"What is your plan for dealing with the Dark Caster?" Areleus asked.

Keeping a careful eye on his father, Dominic removed the wards on the book and picked it up. Sabin stood taller, shifting his posture to a defensive stance while also keeping a keen eye on Areleus. He received a less conspicuous attentive gaze from Ileana. And from my vantage point, from Anand. Uniforms blurred past the open door. Guards. Areleus's guards had been sent away. Although they were the estate's guards, their loyalty was to Areleus.

"Is it safe to assume I will not be involved in this plan?" Areleus asked.

"It isn't necessary, but your participation would be appreciated. I will be in a vulnerable state, which I hope you won't take advantage of."

Areleus was on high alert. The wards were down, and as Dominic flipped through the book, moving from behind the desk to gather objects in the room, including an obsidian knife with writing engraved on the blade, Areleus attempted to look disinterested. It was a struggle. Several times he had to rip his gaze from the Book of Umbra. He directed his attention to the office, moving throughout it as if it was his first visit. A lot of attention was devoted to the books on the shelves.

His indecipherable expression made it difficult to determine if it was an exploratory perusal or if he knew exactly what he was looking for. Were there other things hidden from him and he was taking the opportunity to take them, or get a better layout of the bookshelves to take something later?

I pressed my lips together to keep the frown from etching its way onto my face as I continued to grapple with the realization that each of these men intended to murder the other to claim the throne. I wished Emoni was with me. At least I'd have the comfort of knowing that I wasn't the odd one in this house of weirdness because I seemed to be the only one disturbed by it. But although I'd love to have her with me, I was happy she was sheltered from this.

Minutes ticked by, the silence only heightening the interest in the room. Ileana, Areleus, Sabin, and Anand all kept a keen eye on Dominic.

Anand split his attention between a hyperaware Areleus and Dominic. Dominic placed a spherical object, a crystal filled with a bluish substance, and the obsidian blade on his desk. He kept hold of the Book of Umbra.

His gaze shifted from the items on his desk to Areleus.

"The animosity between us ends today," he said.

A rose streak lined the bridge of Ileana's nose and the hollows of her cheek. Her fingers dug deep into the arm of the chair, threatening to puncture the material. Dominic gave his mother a tight, apologetic smile.

"If things are successful, I still won't be in a position to have the power or influence to demand compliance of the supernaturals, or to enforce it in the same manner I had before." He nudged the spherical object toward his mother.

"This realm needs to be protected, and it's only a matter of time before Helena's magic is used to find a pathway here. They want Luna, and I won't let that happen."

Dominic's concession took Areleus's focus away from the book and placed it firmly on Dominic, assessing him for deceit or alternative plans.

Ileana's clenched jaw indicated she was waiting for an explanation.

"I will be using this to rid them of their magic, but it can't be done without the sacrifice of mine. *Some* of mine," he added to stop the objection Ileana was about to make. "I'm going to use the *clyrin* spell, which will bind my magic along with theirs to this." He pointed to the spherical object. "Then it will be destroyed."

"How?" Ileana asked.

"A different spell. I'm counting on you to do it. I don't think I will be in a position to do so," he admitted.

"Then there is no way I'd ever do it."

"You want Helena back. I will achieve that. The Dark Casters will be without magic and no longer a threat." He looked at me. "No longer a threat because they will no longer have the magical ability to be a threat. The spell demands a sacrifice of magic. Once the sphere is destroyed, so is the magic."

"And they continue to be allowed to live after forcing you into a magical castration?" she snapped. "Do you think they won't become more of a nuisance? If you make that sacrifice, it should not be without some penalty other than just the loss of their magic."

"They will be imprisoned. Living without their magic will be worse than death for them."

"You'd do this to yourself for what?" she snapped again and lobbed a sharp glare in my direction.

Before I could point out that this was my first time hearing the plan, Dominic spoke. "Not for her. For peace. I won't be without magic, but it will not be at the same level as before."

"And you are okay with that?" Areleus asked in a heavy voice.

Dominic's brand of casual arrogance reared. "I conceded not because I fear that I'd be weak but because it won't be just my magic sacrificed. This will be as well." He raised the book.

Areleus moved quickly. Claws exposed, he lunged for the Book of Umbra. The book disappeared from Dominic's hand.

"Stop," Ileana demanded. Standing, she snatched up the

obsidian knife and pricked her finger. After whispering a few words, her long fingers caressed the air, creating a diaphanous map with illuminated gold plots over it. Closing her eyes, she moved over each inch of it, her breathing becoming increasingly rapid with her agitation.

She struck the map away.

"Do you think I didn't try a location spell to find her?" Areleus asked.

"It was worth another attempt," she retorted.

A flicker of tenderness softened Dominic's expression. In that moment, Ileana's profound sense of helplessness washed over the room, an emotion he likely hadn't witnessed before in her. A raw fragility that made me sideline all her past transgressions and violent suggestions. Power was more than just lust and a drive for more. It wrapped them in security that left them ill prepared for upheavals that were beyond their control.

"You're sure this will work?" she asked. "There is no room for error or speculation."

"I'm sure it will, but you will need to do the spell."

Opening his hand, the Book of Umbra materialized. He opened it to a particular page before handing it to her. Rooted in place, a range of anger and frustration flashed over Areleus's face.

"You must do this spell quickly. If they manage to get the orb before it is destroyed, they'll have access to my magic and theirs. You know how nebulous magic can be. Sometimes it can create things we haven't seen before."

Anand came to my mind.

She nodded absently, pulled into her thoughts.

"If that happens, they may gain the ability to navigate through our realm unchecked. After this spell, the Dark Casters will be as vulnerable as humans. They will live the remainder of their lives in the Perils without magic," Dominic asserted.

"The remaining shades, will they be returned?" Areleus asked with the guise of restoring order when we all knew he wanted to be the one to control the shades. With the Book of Umbra destroyed, he was less likely to get that wish, but I doubted he'd give up trying to find a way. If the Book of Umbra existed, I suspected there was something equally terrible that just hadn't been discovered yet.

Dominic considered his question. "There is a way to subdue and control them. After this, I won't have the power to do so."

"Then destroy them now," Ileana said. "Be done with the issue or the prospect of another escape. Celeste is still alive because you've remained persistent in honoring your agreement with the witches. I assure you, her demise would make things easier. It is the most pragmatic thing to do. The strongest witches will no longer be of concern. The others..." She waved her hand, dismissing the other magic wielders with the same derision and disregard she held for humans. "I still don't understand why you negotiate with them. This mutual regard is off-putting."

Ileana's eyes briefly slipped to the door, where Emoni had meandered in without being stopped by Anand. Probably considered more of an annoyance than a threat, she had more freedom than the guards.

Catching the tail end of Ileana's comment, Emoni's face scrunched into an expression of irritation.

She inched toward Ileana, but Anand fisted her shirt, limiting her movement.

"Why are you like this? In fact, why are any of you like this?" She asked the question with deep-seated curiosity. She'd heard more than I'd thought. There seemed to be a desperate need to discover the psychosis or trauma that led these people to be this way. As if being who they were was unacceptable to her. The spark of curiosity demanded answers.

When it was left unanswered, she repeated the question. "Why?" Her head snapped in Dominic's direction. "Not you. You're not totally terrible. But you two"—she stabbed a finger at Areleus and Ileana—"you two are..." She huffed, seemingly searching for the right word. "Your beliefs are unconscionable. Stop letting annihilation be the answer to everything. You don't seem to consider the long-term consequences. You're not hated because of the power you wield. It's because of your abuse of that power."

Neither one seemed at all moved by the pitiful human's outburst. There appeared to be mutual amusement that eventually led to them dismissing her question with a smirk.

"Is there a spell to take away magic from everyone? It seems like it's more trouble than it is helpful?" Emoni asked Dominic. He looked entertained rather than irritated.

"Magic will always exist in some form," he answered. "It can't be wiped away, which is why the magic must be transferred to a magical object capable of holding it, and then destroyed. There's nothing that could remove all the magic from the world because there are so many varying types. There's not a spell to stop vampirism. You can kill vampires on sight with a spell, but not everyone has the magical ability to do so. I've never tried it. I've always preferred a more direct way of handling them."

She glared. "Do you want to stay on the 'alright, possibly decent' list?" she snapped back. "I'll take you off it right now."

Emoni had no idea how little they cared about being considered likable or decent.

"I think you value honesty most of all. I'm giving it to you," he responded.

"Your answer isn't the right one." The frustration and hostility drained from her tone. She appeared bewildered and tired. Shouldn't I be, too? It was bothersome that I may have adapted to this world. I didn't want that to happen.

"I doubt you'd continue this unwavering support and advocacy if you were aware of how you'd be treated if vampires were left to their own wishes. You're beautiful. Vampires would keep you for food and sexual satisfaction. No rules would keep them from compelling you to behave as they wished." Ileana was pleased by Emoni's fearful retreat to her spot next to Anand, who appeared to have become her safe haven. "Shifters would demand that you abide by their ways, which are dogmatic at best and subjugating at worst. Witches would use their magic to make humans into puppets and servants. Be cautious about giving any of them your meritless loyalty. They aren't a trouble for you humans because we've made it so."

Emoni looked at me, her face reflecting what I felt: a desperation to leave and return to our world of blissful ignorance. Though it would be pseudo bliss because we were now aware of the machinations that existed behind it. How fragile the peace really was. Just one broken oath, rogue supernatural, or organized and well-orchestrated revolt could end it all.

Being with me and seeing it all unfold may have been some comfort to her, but I was doubtful that harsh reality was an adequate trade-off. Anand's eyes grazed over the room and back to a dispirited Emoni beside him. His hand pressed into her back, guiding her out of the room, which she accepted meekly.

Dominic continued explaining the plan. It hinged on me allowing the bespelled knot to do its job and bring me to the Dark Casters. I was less uneasy about it than Dominic, who tensed each time he mentioned it.

The last time he brought it up, to comfort him, I directed his attention to my arm that now had a cloaked binding on it. A location spell.

"I will be with Luna, who will have the Diax." He handed me the spherical object. I didn't blame him for splitting everything up. It made it difficult for Areleus to get access to them all.

Areleus kept his eyes glued to the Book of Umbra, which was now in Ileana's possession. With the wards removed from it, I wondered if it was safe—or if she was safe from Areleus. She left the room with a watchful Sabin. Something was different about him now. The playful amorphized creature had a menacing aura that screamed danger. I didn't believe for one minute that it wasn't without cause. And the reason he stayed at Ileana's side.

13

After leaving his office, Dominic accompanied me while I searched for Emoni. I found her in the library, curled up in one of the oversized chairs, a highball glass on the table next to her, and engrossed in a book. She looked relaxed and that was a comfort. A little less reassuring was that the day had reduced her to drunk reading. This would be over soon. I relaxed more than expected despite the ominous hum that lingered in the house and the feeling that I was always being watched, which was highly likely. I welcomed Dominic's retreat to his suite.

Closing the door, he pressed me against the wall, his face inches from mine. Fierce eyes connected with mine.

"There is always a chance that things could go awry and you could be placed in danger. You should change your mind."

"Make things more difficult for you? I'm not going to allow anyone to hurt me." The bravado almost led me to believe it. Like I had dormant magic waiting to be used.

"If I manage to fail, then you'll be a good back-up plan, right?" A teasing smile curled his lips but didn't reach his eyes. I saw the traces of uncertainty in them. His attempt to lighten the mood didn't work.

"You're taking a huge risk for a group who would not do the same to save your life," he said.

"I'm aware of that. If this will mitigate the chaos and make things easier for you, I'll do it. And it will save Helena." She was his sister and despite it all, he cared about her despite the warranted anger and hostility he had for her. "You're making a bigger sacrifice than I am. Are you prepared for not having the same advantage you had before?" Seeing the royals' reaction to this situation and how even the smallest feelings of helplessness unraveled them, how would he deal with not wielding magic as he once had? I took hold of his hand, examining his long fingers that in seconds could turn into deadly sharp weapons. "Will you have these?"

He looked down at his fingers. My reference caused him to extend his claws. Examining them, he shook his head. "Probably not. It would be different, and a challenge, if I was to actually lose my magic."

"What?" I fumbled out. I knew damn well I just sat in the I'm-going-to-sacrifice-my magic-to-end-this-and-concede-to-my-father meeting. What the hell did I miss?

He nibbled at the bottom of my lips. Retracting his claws, deft fingers slid over my back, unfastening my bra that he quickly discarded. Returning to move under my shirt, his fingers glided over my skin until they came to the swell of my breasts. His thumb stroked and teased my nipples until they hardened. Ducking down, he took one into his mouth, his tongue laving and teasing as his magic curled around me in a sensual caress and once again tethering magic and sex together. A moan escaped as I responded, feeling him all over me. The need for satisfaction spread over me, settling between my legs. Delivering the same treatment to the other breast, he clouded my mind with thoughts of feeling him inside me.

I fought through the distraction, fisted his hair, and guided his face to meet mine. "What do you mean you're not losing your magic?" I asked Dominic, whose eyes and fingers crawled over my body, giving me hints of all the erotic things going through his mind. "What did I miss?" Because that was a big miss.

"Nothing. Everything I told you is correct, and there will be a sacrifice of magic. It just won't be mine. My father will be his own undoing."

Before I could ask more questions, his mouth covered mine in a heated, hungry kiss while his hand migrated down my stomach, the graze of his nails over my skin sending a shudder through me. When he pulled away, he studied me with a smirk. My unsated curiosity had managed to peek its way through lust. His hand's trail over my body didn't stop, moving into my pants, between my legs. Locking his eyes with mine as his expert fingers moved over my excited nub. My short pants of breath skimmed over his lips that rested lightly against mine.

"I know you are curious, and I would like you to know more, but nothing can be given away. Nothing." His fingers slipped into me and I moaned, arching into the touch, my head pressing against the wall. "Can you trust me, Luna?" His fingers moving inside me, I rocked my hips to meet each thrust. Each brush of his fingers over my aroused clit brought me to new heights of pleasure, a burgeoning climax I was desperate for.

"Yes." It came out in a throaty rasp to both his question and to the explosive climax he gave me. Laced with my desire was trust. I did trust him. And I loved him. And thoroughly enjoyed sex with him.

I pressed a delicate kiss to his lips that started off as a sweet and tender connection that escalated to more. His hands roved over my body until they were at my breasts, caressing and teasing my nipples until they beaded so tightly they ached.

Threading my fingers into his hair, I pulled him to me, kissing him deeply while my other hand slipped under his shirt, his tantalizing heat warming my fingers. Coursing down his abs to the button on his pants. His pants slid down, and when he stepped out of them, I took his silky girth into my hands, stroking it until it came to its full hardness. Holding his tumultuous gaze, I lowered to my knees and ran my tongue along it, earning a throaty groan from him. He laced his fingers through my hair, his desperate pants encouraging as I took him in my mouth, my tongue running underside with a slow glide over the length of him. His deep growls of pleasure filled the room, slow thrusts meeting my movements.

Guiding me to stand, his eyes glittered with dark hunger. He lifted me; my legs curled around his waist.

"Luna," he murmured with reverence, carrying me through the suite until we made it to his bed where he laid me down. Closing his eyes, he inhaled a slow breath and took even longer to exhale. When he opened them, there was a roiling of heated emotions. As he completed removing my shirt, his nails grazed my skin. I shivered at the contact. He delivered the same treatment to my pants, delivering erotic tantalizing kisses to the sensitive area around my thighs and between my legs. My body became a coil of heat that missed the contact of his skin when he moved from me. Hastily, he tugged his shirt off, sending buttons sprawling. He discarded the ripped shirt. He showed little regard for his pants, but they stayed intact as he ripped them from his body. Dominic reared back, a ravenous roving of his eyes taking me all in, like a feast he was ready to devour.

Claiming my mouth with another kiss, he settled between my legs, guiding his cock into me with a groan of satisfaction. His movements slow and deep, my fingers digging into his back. Meeting his intensified movements, more rapacious. A desperate need to find that sensual pleasure. Each thrust and movement brought me closer. My hips rocked against him, frenetic energy moving between us. Pulling him to me in a ravenous kiss, I found that pleasure with a shudder and a groan against his lips. With fervent desperation, he inched deeper until he climaxed. Easing out of me, he rested his head against my stomach.

I was starting to drift off in a blissful satisfied nap, when Ileana walked into the bedroom with a flourish of movement, extinguishing my post-orgasmic quiescence as I jolted into a panicked grab for something to cover my body. Unbothered by our nudity, her attention jetted from me to Dominic, who only had curled some of the duvet over him.

"I hope your dalliance sated your frustrations and cleared your head. Have you rethought your plan?" Ileana asked.

"It remains the same." He ran his fingers through his hair, mussing it more than I had.

Her lips pinched. "Do you think it is wise for me to keep the Book of Umbra and not have it under the same protection?"

There was an emptiness on his face, but his eyes were expressive, snagging his mother's attention which had drifted toward me as I made a spectacle of myself gathering my clothes and trying to make an inconspicuous escape to the bathroom. I failed. I slumped next to Dominic, my discarded shirt pressed against my chest but barely covering the areas I wanted covered.

Her eyes fluttered with annoyance. Yes, I quickly discovered I wasn't as oblivious about people seeing me nude as I thought. Even though it was just a body, I didn't want his mother seeing mine.

"No. If Areleus manages to get hold of it, I'm confident it will be returned so we can proceed. Let's not worry about that. He wants Helena back and the Casters dealt with."

I couldn't understand how he could assert that with such a level of unwavering confidence.

Ileana held Dominic's gaze, her look eerie, making me feel as though they were having a silent conversation. There was definitely an understanding that I'd never know. From one look, could she decipher his plan? Admittedly envious of the connection, I reminded myself I had committed to trust him and his plan, although it would have been easier if I knew all the details. He seemed to be withholding some aspects from us all.

"Fine. I'll return to my room and wait." There was an underlying meaning to her response. I figured it was to wait until Areleus tried to get the book. "I suspect he will try to charm me into looking at the book, since he's never had a chance before," she said. "I guess I should allow that to happen."

Dominic offered a small nod. They both held a cunning dark smile that highlighted the familial similarities.

With a small, satisfied chuckle, she left the room.

omic's eyes were drawn to my image in the full-length mirror. The mid-length bodycon dress, one-sleeve style, and modal fabric accentuated the curves of my body and Dominic had taken notice. His gaze trailed from the simple heels, my legs, the fabric stretching over my hips and ass, to my breasts and exposed shoulder, where he placed a kiss before continuing his exploration to my hair, which was pulled back into a loose twist. The dress complemented his gunmetal button-down shirt and black slacks.

"What's with the frown?" he asked. I hadn't noticed the deep creased expression. I relaxed it and turned to face him.

"Why are we dressing for dinner? It has a last meal feel to it," I admitted. When I left Emoni, who'd decided to return to her room, Dominic had asked me to choose between four dresses for dinner. It reminded me that I hadn't eaten.

"Or it could be a new beginnings dinner."

I didn't want to be doom and gloom and tried to let his optimism ease my worry.

The dress and a formal dinner brought to mind memories of Areleus threatening to kill me when I was used as a pawn to force Dominic's hand. I had no desire to return to the scene of the incident.

"We're eating in the other dining room."

I slid my fingers over the front of his shirt. "Was it that obvious?"

He leaned down and kissed me. "I'd prefer a restaurant, but I don't want to take any risks until tomorrow."

Seated next to him, I was delighted to see Emoni and Anand already at the table. I bit back my laughter when Emoni stood up to greet me with a hug and whispered, "I'm keeping this dress."

Dust pink satin skimmed the delicate curves of her tall, slender body. The cinched waist and draping cowl neckline accentuated her body and complemented her height and long lean legs in a way that was difficult to ignore. Anand seemed to be having that problem.

Hungrier than expected, I cut my admiration of the stunning room. Floor-to-ceiling windows offered a view outside. The dark backdrop wasn't as depressing while I devoured beef tenderloin with Périgourdine sauce, potato au gratin, and sautéed mixed vegetables. My hunger wasn't making the food taste more exceptional than it was, because Emoni was taking slow appreciative bites of the meal, occasionally giving me a worried look that she tamped down with sips of wine.

"This is delicious. One would think it's a last meal," she said nervously, a slight tremble in her hand as she brought the wine glass to her lips.

Dominic looked across the table at her and then back to me. "I'm constantly provided with reasons why you all are so close," he said. "Don't see it as an end but rather a beginning."

"What a beautiful sentiment," said Areleus, entering the dining area from the opposite end of the room. Areleus's presence was a surprise, but Callum, the tattooed Seer, next to him was shocking. The ease with which these people switched sides was off-putting.

My heart skipped at their intrusion. Annoyance washed over Dominic's face. Fist clenched, his growl of anger echoed in the intimate space. He cast a furious glance at Callum before standing, stopping his advance.

"Why is he here?" he asked Areleus.

"To settle my worries. With such a dangerous spell, I am concerned about the outcome." Areleus's wolfish smile belied his words.

"Nailah wasn't available?"

Callum smirked, his eyes flickering with amusement. "Nailah is indisposed, unfortunately. But don't worry, I'm more than capable."

Dominic's jaw tensed, the tension in the room thickened, and I couldn't help but wonder if Nailah had been deemed of no use. I didn't believe Areleus would hurt her, but I'd grown conditioned to expect the unexpected.

"So, shall you put my mind at ease and allow him to get a peek into what the future holds?" Areleus asked, attempting to sidestep Dominic, who pushed him back and pinned Callum with a warning look.

At Emoni's confusion and discomfort, Anand leaned into her and whispered something. Hopefully an explanation of what was going on. I'd told her about Seers, but with the influx of so much new information, I couldn't imagine her being able to keep it all straight.

"Where is Nailah?"

"Safe, of course," Areleus snapped at the accusation in Dominic's tone. "Her fondness for you makes her unreliable."

A dangerous glint flashed in Dominic's eyes. Displaying his adept control, his hand closed around Callum's neck, claws extended enough to press into the skin but not break it. Emoni's shocked gasp poured over the room.

Locking eyes with his father, he said, "What do you see, Callum?"

"Let him go, Dominic," Areleus demanded. "Or is this overreaction a deception being revealed?"

"Deception?" He released his hold on Callum who pressed his hand to his neck and stumbled back a few steps, panting for breath. Skewering Dominic with a glare, he put more distance between them.

"Yes, deception." The dark ominous cast in Areleus's expression faded to a falsely gentle one. "I fear that the vulnerable position you are putting yourself in could be exploited. Or worse, you could die. I want Callum to see your future and that of your—" His eyes slid in my direction. I knew "human" was on the tip of his tongue, but one look from Dominic and he decided against it. "Luna."

"Callum already predicted our demise and it didn't happen."

"Helena was taken. We have no confirmation that his sight hasn't come true." The hitch in his voice was the first time Areleus had expressed a human emotion.

"What do you want to know?" Callum asked.

"Tomorrow, what do you see of this place, my son, and Luna?"

Callum stopped massaging his neck and closed his eyes before opening them to reveal his peculiar illuminated violet eyes. His body shuddered slightly before he blinked several times. Shaking his head, he furrowed his brows. The glow of his eyes returned and stayed longer than before, and when they returned to their normal color, confusion swept over his face.

"Nothing. I don't see a future, just the present as things are now. This has never happened before." Callum's suspicious narrowed eyes moved between Areleus and Dominic. He frowned. "Whatever you plan to do tomorrow either has too many variables for me to see an outcome, or the magic is powerful enough to obscure my vision. That's never happened before. If it's able to do that, should you be using it?"

Ignoring Callum's question, Areleus's quick steps ate up the distance between Dominic and him. "What happens if the Diax isn't destroyed?"

"That's not an option. If you want Helena back, to protect this realm, and to end the existence of the Dark Casters' magic, it has to be destroyed," Dominic rebutted.

"It's such a waste to destroy magic that could be used."

"At the cost of Helena and our future safety?" Dominic asked.

After a few minutes of studying Dominic, Areleus seemed to have come to a concession.

"Of course. It seemed as if you're in such a rush to protect Luna that you may be using extreme measures. I guess not."

He beckoned for Callum to follow him out. Dominic kept a careful eye on them as they exited.

We returned to our dinner, but I couldn't enjoy it what with Callum's concerns that nagged at me, Emoni's worry returning in full force, and Dominic's distracted attention that had him staring out the window with a frown. Areleus was curious, and that made him more of a wild card.

"Is everything okay?" I whispered.

Dominic turned to face me. The intensity of his look was an intimate pull that made it feel like we were the only ones in the room. His finger trailed lightly over my cheek.

"Of course it is."

Even with all the uncertainty I felt, there was one thing I was sure of: Dominic was lying to me.

Once we were alone after dinner, I asked Dominic if he had prevented Callum from using his ability to see the tomorrow's outcome. He said he hadn't and Ileana denied doing it as well. Neither one seemed bothered by the incident, but I couldn't stop thinking about it. He saw things as they were at that moment. I took it as a portentous message.

For hours, rushes of dark thought warded off sleep. When I turned to my left, Dominic's eyes were open and he was studying me with curiosity. A small inquiring smile curled his lips as his finger traced my cheekbone.

"Nailah or the vision?" Dominic whispered.

"What?"

"Which one is keeping you up, my father not consulting Nailah or Callum's vision?"

"He didn't have a vision. He didn't see anything. Why doesn't that bother you?"

"A Seer's divinations aren't infallible and are susceptible to the actions of others. I explained to you that my plan is nebulous, constantly evolving. I'm sure the same is true with my father. Callum is not as skilled as Nailah, so it's not surprising that he wasn't able to see anything."

"Then shouldn't we consult with Nailah?" I really wanted to know our fate, or at least something other than the present, because to me, it meant we didn't have a future.

Dominic rolled out of bed. After a few minutes in the bathroom, he gathered his clothing and dressed in a pair of jeans and a T-shirt that molded to his muscles. He rarely dressed so casually, and it was a look that suited him.

He smirked. "Are you going to get dressed or stare?"

"Both," I teased, getting out of bed. Quickly, I got ready in jeans with a soft peach-colored V-neck T-shirt.

"We need to be careful. I'm doing this to ease your mind because I don't want the weight of this to compromise your safety tomorrow." His eyes flicked to the clock. "Or rather, later today," he said. It was a few minutes past midnight and we were going to visit Nailah. I'd never consider visiting someone at this time, but I really needed answers.

Moments later, we stood on the porch of a charming white farmhouse. The porch boasted a white railing delicately carved with intricate patterns. A pair of rattan rocking chairs with light green cushions made the house seem welcoming and comfortable. Flowers decorated the area near the door, infusing the air with their sweet fragrance.

The door opened and Nailah greeted us with an expectant look. She was dressed in a soft-looking lilac waffle knit lounge set. Her braids were secured by a patterned scarf. She might have expected our visit, but she was definitely dressed for a relaxing night at home. I felt remorseful for keeping her from it.

Stepping inside, the interior of the house was as equally warm and welcoming as the exterior. I'm sure it was intentional. When your gift is seeing the future, the good along with the bad, and tasked with revealing it to others, I'd want my home to be a place of serenity.

Following her into the living room, my senses were lulled by the tranquil white walls and hints of eucalyptus wafting in the air. Large plants were placed in the corners of the room, various potted plants around the griege-colored cloud-like sofa, and a rounded airy lounger surrounded a ragged-shaped teak table. Large statement art placed throughout her home managed to be both stunning and unobtrusive.

Nailah sank into the airy round lounger and invited us to sit on the sofa. Dominic laced his hand with mine. Nailah's eyes shifted to our hands then lifted to meet Dominic's, offering him a wide smile.

"What brings you here?" she asked.

"Callum visited us in the Underworld."

Her brows inched together and her mouth parted. Confusion flitted over her expression.

"Areleus extended an invitation to him," Dominic provided.

His answer didn't quell her curiosity. "Why Callum?"

Dominic exhaled a long breath. "I plan to use the Book of Umbra and the Diax to remove the magic from the remaining Dark Casters," he told her. "Sacrificing my magic to complete the spell. The Book of Umbra will be destroyed in the process."

Nailah whooshed like the breath had been knocked out of her. She sat with the information for a while before asking, "I still don't understand why Callum was there in my place?" Hurt broke through her curiosity.

"You coddle me too much." Dominic smirked at Areleus's implication. "He didn't trust that you'd give him impartial information."

"Was he worried about your survival from the spell?" she asked.

A sheepish half smile curled her lips at Dominic's incredulous scowl in response. "I suppose he wanted to confirm that my magic would be diminished and that no alternative motives were in play."

"But there are, aren't they?"

He nodded, then gave her an abridged version of the plan. Me being used to find the Dark Casters, his mother performing the spell with the Diax, and his magic being the sacrifice for the spell to work. "I ask that you trust me and don't ask for further information."

"What did Callum see?"

"Nothing. He said he couldn't see anything but the present."

After a few minutes of consideration, she offered him a small nod. "Don't die."

"I don't plan to."

She didn't seem as confident as Dominic. Standing, she came to us, then knelt, her touch comforting as it covered our clasped hands. Warm brown eyes flowed into luminous violet as she stared past us. Minutes ticked by. She made several attempts. Confusion and fear lingered in her face and eyes when they returned to their natural color. Returning to her chair, she remained quiet while she processed whatever she saw.

"Is the Book of Umbra still warded?"

"No. I removed it and my mother has it."

Nailah's face became a blank landscape and her eyes flattened to an expressionless pool of warm brown. "Ileana has it. You have no concerns about that?" If he didn't, she definitely did, and now I did as well. She knew Ileana better than I did. But Dominic seemed to be an expert when it came to understanding his parents. They were his parents and his decisions could be biased.

"No," he said with a confidence I no longer possessed. My mind descended into a number of possible outcomes and fear raced through me. Dominic's hand covered mine and when I turned to him, his eyes latched on to mine. "Please keep your trust in me."

I nodded and ushered away the doubt and the negative thoughts that drowned out the hint of optimism I had allowed and the promise that it would all be over soon.

"You do the same," he urged Nailah.

"The Book of Umbra should have been destroyed when you got possession of it. It's a powerful book. I believe because it is no longer warded by your magic, it has formed its own barrier of protection preventing it from being found by anyone else. It is doubtful anyone would be able to see the outcome of its use. I just hope it will be a success."

When she stood, we did as well at her tacit invitation to end the visit.

I doubted she'd return to her leisurely evening. Flashes of concern fell and reasserted themselves over the small tight smile she offered as she moved to the door. Before Dominic could leave, she placed a hand on his arm.

"Don't kill your father," she entreated.

He studied her for a long time, but I don't think he understood her intent. I gathered it wasn't a plea to save Areleus, but rather Dominic.

His hand covered hers, a calming veneration in his tone as he addressed her. "Whether he lives or dies is solely up to him. I hope he chooses well."

He searched her face as if looking for an answer that never came. Offering her a humorless smile, he gave his departing goodbye. Pulling me to him, we returned to his home.

15

The next morning, the visit with Nailah had only intensified my worries about the potential dystopian outcomes, undermining Dominic's constant reassurance of our success. Jittery and on edge, the three hours we took to prepare for the spell dragged.

Hoping my demeanor showed more confidence and less skepticism than I felt, I'd still caught Dominic giving me assessing looks several times. I hadn't fooled him. I was a discord of emotions, the most prominent of which was fear. The more I thought of the many things that could go wrong, the more my fear grew. I wasn't in a hurry to come face to face with two Dark Casters. Sheathed at my leg was a knife, which Anand had displayed an exceptional level of optimism giving to me. I clipped the pepper spray Emoni brought with her onto the top of my pants. My shirt was long enough to hide it. No matter how powerful you might be, pepper spray in the eye was a good deterrent and a good equalizer. Unfortunately, if you're able to use pepper spray on a person, they're too close for comfort.

Areleus held on to the Book of Umbra, his face an unreadable slate. I couldn't help but recall Callum's look of

141

confusion that he'd seen nothing. Watching Areleus's confident stride and protective hold on the Book of Umbra as he moved throughout the room, there was something I couldn't quite pinpoint. It only added to my uncertainty as to whether he would relinquish the book or let it get destroyed because he had other plans. No one else seemed to have the same concern. Perhaps they figured he'd had enough time with the book to have copied or committed to memory the spells he wanted.

I attempted to adopt the veneer of cool indifference that hung heavily in the room. The surety etched on their faces and effortless movements should have emboldened me, but instead I was nagged by the persistent feeling that being overconfident ensured that whatever could go wrong, would. Dominic putting so much faith in how his father would be his own undoing was a variable I didn't like. *Trust him*, I reminded myself. Ileana was trusting him and we had only been given parts of the plan. Areleus would be the sacrifice.

Pushing aside my doubts, I returned Emoni's hug, assuring her that everything would be fine. It didn't stop the various ways she cajoled and demanded I be careful, before she returned to the other side of the house with Anand, who kept a safe distance between me and the bespelled infinity knot. He planned to meet us at my apartment, after taking Emoni home. Steadfast in her objection to stay with me, she finally conceded when I pointed out that she was another body to protect or one to be used for retaliation or bait.

Anand stood several feet from me, holding the bespelled infinity knot. In Dominic's home, when the knot wasn't in my vicinity, I forgot how torrid the magic felt.

"Are you okay?" he asked, and I pulled my focus from the object in Anand's hand to him.

I shook my head. If vampire compulsion was anything like this, no one stood a chance. The unbearable ache reached deep to my bones. My fingers tingled and it took everything for me not to grab for it. Closing my eyes, I sucked in a breath and counted backward. It did absolutely nothing. My body craved to take a running leap at the object and take whatever it had to offer. I opened my eyes at the eclipse of darkness I'd sensed, to see Dominic standing in front of me.

"You're doing great," he whispered, his lips inches from mine. I fell into the pools of amber in his eyes, allowing them to consume my thoughts.

"I'm so done with magic when this is over. I will never try to satisfy my curiosity again. I might not even read another book," I pledged.

His low rumble of laughter redirected my ache for the object to him. "I'm magic. I won't let you be through with me."

"Not you. That's different." The words rang true because they were, but so did the reality of my existence.

Lifting my chin he studied me, the smile leaving his eyes. Face to face, I forgot we were in the room with Anand, Areleus, and Ileana. It was an intimate moment. Just the two of us, the world falling away.

"Do you wonder what I really am?" I asked.

"You're my Luna. That's all that matters." Once the spell was over and Dark Caster magic destroyed, I was Luna. A different version of Luna. A post Dark Caster magic wielder and a world of chaos, violence, and strife left behind. That Luna was going to be a hell of a lot more cynical. How could she not be?

I nodded, finding some comfort in his words although the unanswered questions remained.

"I need you to be careful. If there was another way, I would have chosen it," Dominic whispered.

Maybe I was too naive, but Ophelia wanted me, so I didn't feel like my life was in jeopardy. More than likely, I'd be annoyed by her pandering and speeches of persuasion or disgusted by her plans.

Taking hold of the bespelled infinity knot, magic laced around me, no longer a tug. It secured my fingers to it, which shook from the force of it and the magic that pulsed through me. Meeting Dominic's gaze, outwardly I exhibited a bravado that was being whittled away by the second into a chaotic maelstrom.

My optimism quickly escalated to anxiety in equal measure when the knot emitted a vibrant glow that punched more magic into the room. Alone. Panic crowded out all other emotions. All the discussions hadn't prepared me for the immense loneliness of facing Peter and Ophelia alone, or the creativity of my thoughts as they conjured more harmful scenarios. What if the royals were unable to break any of the wards Ophelia had created? After all, she had avoided capture for years. And was powerful enough to snatch my magic with magic alone. No objects to assist her. What if the locating spell Dominic placed on me failed? Or as revenge for punching her, Ophelia threw out any plans of having me as an ally and decided to kill me? Ophelia killing me was unlikeliest of them all. Doubt became like a persistent shadow, lingering in my psyche.

"Luna." Ophelia's expression matched her satin melodious voice that welcomed me. "What brings you here?"

Is she screwing with me? One look around the room confirmed my visit was expected, and the mood was set for it. Heavy terra cotta curtains blocked out any hint of light or any way to reveal the proximity of neighbors, if there were any. This was a house, I was sure of it. I stood in the middle of a living room. The open floor plan gave me a full view of a modern kitchen, a sitting room, and a section of the home that had been designated as a library. The bookcase held more objects and talismans than books. The midnight-gray walls could easily be mistaken for wallpaper instead of paint, and the sigils and glyphs covering every inch of it created a macabre pattern that could have lent to a gothic décor. My heart thrashed against my chest. Would they disrupt the location spell?

Slowly turning, I took in the full view and possible exits. The curtains covered what I assumed was a sliding door exit in the kitchen. To get to the front door, I'd have to get past Ophelia. I looked for things that could be used as a weapon. I got sight of a vase, a computer on the coffee table, a ceramic bowl on the table against the wall, and a few decorative items that didn't quite fit the dark décor.

"I got your invitation," I said, opening my hand to reveal the magic object and shooting a glance to my right where Peter was perched in a chair next to a dispirited Helena. She looked physically fine and had no noticeable restraints. My overactive mind created the scenario of another betrayal, until I saw the sigils laced around her fingers. Similar ones decorated Peter and Ophelia's fingers. I couldn't determine what had made her eyes glassy, but she was losing the fight to keep back tears. One emotion was obvious whenever her eyes drifted in either Peter's or Ophelia's direction: a thirst for retaliation.

"I wish it was an invitation that you'd accepted alone." She tossed a look in Peter's direction and he stood. He joined her in making rote movements of their hands while their lips moved at a fervent pace, casting a spell. With a final swiping hand movement, the markings on the walls became white illuminations of bars that stretched over all the walls in the room. Where there wasn't a wall, a network of lines formed, attaching to the bars. Fear blazed in me at the sight of them.

Once again, I was imprisoned. It seemed like my concerns were warranted.

"I'm locked in," I said softly.

She smiled. "You're not locked in. They're just locked out."

"Is there a difference?"

"To me there is. The same as lying low and refusing to be hunted." A dark sneer made it to her eyes. "They're here. Too bad there was a small part of me that wanted to believe in you." She turned to Peter. "You were right, she is enthralled by *him*. She will never align with us." Cool, disapproving eyes traveled over me and snagged on the cross purse where I'd stored the Diax. Nothing could be done without Dominic and Ileana.

The bars around us wavered and shimmered in a gallant effort to stay intact. Worry crept over Peter's face while he watched the attack on their ward. Ophelia didn't share that same concern; she smirked at whatever the royals were doing on the other side of the house. A thunderous sound snapped my attention to the door. Resounding thuds and pounding were heard from outside.

"They're occupied, for the moment," Ophelia said to what had become her preemptive distraction. Fighting.

The front door pulled away, giving me a view of Dominic just as a wolf lunged at him and a vampire swooped in from another direction. At the sound of bone breaking followed by a shrill, tortured sound that ended abruptly, I was sure with a death, I swallowed down the bile that had arisen.

"Search her," Ophelia commanded of Peter, pulling my attention from my limited view of the commotion outside.

"Don't touch me," I snapped when he moved toward me.

A sneer warped Ophelia's features. Blue whirls of magic danced over her fingertips. "Should I coax you into compliance?" she asked. "I can assure you it won't be pleasant."

Her eyes snapped to the glowing bars that continued to

waver and shake but held. "They despise us because of our magic."

"Don't forget your abuse of it."

"Has his sister been held to the same standards?"

The ragged breath I sucked in served as my answer, because there wasn't any defense for Helena's behavior, and she'd never been held to account for it. She was cruel. She wielded her magic with vengeance and never suffered any penalties for it. Peeling my eyes from Ophelia, I looked at Helena. Crestfallen eyes and her somber appearance showed something I'd never seen on her. Regret. Her glistening eyes dropped to her fingers. I couldn't make out the sigils and it wouldn't be very helpful even if I could. The only thing that made sense was that it was a magical restriction, or they'd figured a way to bind their magic to hers, giving them access to the Underworld.

"What do you have on you, Luna?" Ophelia demanded. As she slowly approached me, the magic that moved over her fingers became more frenetic, bringing back painful memories of my other run-in with her magic. A dark smile flitted over her lips at the grimace the recollection forced.

"Why me?" She was probably the only one who could answer that question. Of all the people in the world, I was the one chosen to carry the magic and to be brought into this chaotic, nefarious world.

"Luck," she said.

"Is it? How so?"

Her lips parted to answer when the bars shook again.

"Ah, you have no interest in the answer. Just more time. For what? What little scheme do they have planned?"

I shook my head. There wasn't an Oscar in my future. "I don't know. Answer my question. Why me?"

Whatever she saw on my face, she sighed. "I'm not sure. Opportunity and desperation to preserve the magic." I got the impression she wished it was someone else, too. Perhaps someone she could have coerced into it. Someone who shared her thirst for domination and to rule the supernatural world without any care for the number of casualties it would take to do so.

Ophelia repeated her question about the contents of my bag. The Diax was too large to put on me or even hold in my hand without looking suspicious. We knew the risk of her thinking something was in the bag rather than it being as simple as part of my outfit. Although it was possible she did believe that and was just being overly diligent.

"Phone, wallet, lip gloss, lotion, an e-reader, and other junk." The Diax was flat enough that it could be hidden among the other items. "Are you really interested in that?" In response to her inching closer to me, I revealed the lip gloss and phone. If that was true, hopefully she'd believe the rest.

Looking at me with skepticism, she made a show of winding her hand back. Shuffling back, I yanked off the purse and tossed it to her feet. Peter snatched it up and took out all the contents, palming the Diax and examining it for several moments. Ophelia split her attention between me and the object.

"What is it for?"

"I don't know. I just had to keep it with me."

"You're a terrible liar," she snapped.

A sentiment that Helena shared. Shaking her head, she sank deeper into the chair and looked at the ceiling, probably aware that any efforts to save her probably just went out the window.

Ophelia quickly closed the distance between us. Glaring at me, she demanded through clenched teeth, "What is it for?"

"I don't know." The magic felt worse than it looked when it came in contact with me, sending throbbing pain and an ache through me. I crumpled to the floor. Tears blurred my vision.

She lowered herself closer. The rings of gold that circled me made my heart race. "What is it for?" she repeated.

I attempted to blink back the tears, but they streamed down my face. "To take your magic. It will be destroyed afterward."

"How is that possible? Anything of that sort requires a sacrifice of magic. Strong magic."

I nodded. "Dominic was making the sacrifice."

"What spell is it?"

At my shrug, she moved the golden magic closer to me. I flinched at the threat. "I don't know. He has it in his office and plans to destroy it afterward."

"You've aligned yourself with the weak. Are you satisfied?" After a long assessing gaze, she frowned. "You've weakened him. People spoke of him with great fear, and he makes this choice?" She scoffed. "You've dulled his edge and compromised him to the point that he will not be feared enough to be of any use."

That was the first time I felt really concerned that she'd kill me. I was no longer viewed as an asset but a liability.

I'd seen the look that passed over her face when she looked at Areleus. Unrestrained yearning. Still palming the Diax, the magic fizzled from her hand. She took hold of my wrist, then nodded in Peter's direction. He closed his eyes, and so did I, in preparation for what I knew would happen.

When I opened my eyes, we were outside the Perils. The only place Peter had been and therefore the only place he could use the magic to travel to. Outside the cells were me, Ophelia, and Peter. They'd left Helena. There wasn't any way Helena would have stayed behind of her own volition.

It was up to me.

16

Ophelia gave the Underworld a once-over, a rueful smile tugging at her lips as she went from cell to cell until she came to the only one occupied. Celeste.

Trying to anticipate her intentions, I thought there were two possibilities: She'd release Celeste and form an alliance with her, or kill her and end the bloodline of the most powerful witches in the world. I was pretty sure it was the latter. Seconds from snatching the pepper spray hooked on my pants, I was able to conceal it from notice when Peter's and Ophelia's attention was drawn to thunderous footsteps descending the stairs. Rushing into the Perils, eight guards entered, swords in hand. Peter smiled at them as if they weren't a threat, making several fierce rote movements. I ducked as black clouds of ether coalesced.

With a simple whisper of a spell, he materialized a mass of arrows. There were too many to count. At another sharp command, the arrows propelled through the air with the lethality of bullets. Agonized sounds reverberated off the walls and bodies thudded. Taking a shuddering breath, I looked back and confirmed the deaths of eight guards in a matter of moments.

"You're a monster," I whispered.

Peter's satisfied smirk wavered, but the insult didn't land or have the effect I wanted. His hands made more sharp movements while he recited another spell. I lunged to the side, bracing for the impact, but nothing happened to me. Out of my periphery, I saw a flare of light cover the stairway.

Where are you all? I feared they were still trying to get past the wards on the house or engaged in the fighting used as a delay tactic. My empathy was running thin for all who sided with Dark Casters.

Peter nodded. No remorse or self-reflection. There had been days when he'd battled with the cognitive dissonance, but he'd given in to power lust.

"I'd rather be the monster than the prey."

That's why Ophelia had returned his magic.

He eased closer to me. I shuffled back.

"What about you, Luna?"

"What?" I was splitting my attention between him and Ophelia, who appeared to be disabling the series of spells that kept Celeste behind bars. Illumination and sparks bled from the cloaked wards. From her intense focus, it wasn't an easy task. Good.

"You realize Dominic and the others will die. You will not have any form of protection. The Conventicle and the Awakeners blame you for starting all this. That"—my eyes followed his to the Diax, which Ophelia had placed on the floor as if it was inconsequential—"means nothing."

Did he know something I didn't? My heart was thrashing with panic when he opened his hand and the Diax soared into his palm. He eyed it, his smirk darkening as he whispered a spell over it. Sparks flickered from the object, and a light field formed around it, protecting itself from Peter's attack. His smirk drained into anger.

While destruction of the Diax had his focus, I said, "Peter."

His eyes flicked up to me and he was assaulted with stinging mist. Pepper spray.

"Fuck," he hissed when the irritant forced him to drop the Diax, which skidded a few inches away. Then I kneed him in his man berries. One hand went for the assaulted area while the other flicked at me, a protective burst of magic that pushed me back several feet. While he recovered, I scooped up the Diax and headed for the stairs, getting another look at the fallen guards. Peter's strained mocking chortle hung in the air as I attempted to escape but smashed into the barrier he'd created. The opaque wall made it difficult to see if more guards were behind it, trying to get in. There had to be another entrance to the Perils.

Peter's laugh cut short into a terrible gurgling. I turned to find Peter held against Dominic, whose claws were pressed into Peter's neck, down which flowed rivulets of blood. A gold band formed around them. Opening my hand, I revealed the Diax to Dominic.

A look of pride and relief broke through his sneer. Ophelia was struggling to keep Ileana and Areleus at bay while still directing her attention to releasing Celeste. I couldn't figure out why releasing Celeste was so important. Did she believe that releasing her would serve as a big enough distraction?

I wasn't sure who was responsible for breaking the ward that kept Ileana and Areleus from Ophelia. Her suffocating rage consumed the room as she turned to face them.

Dominic instructed me to release the Diax. It fell to the floor, setting things in motion.

Ophelia directed her anger at me, whipping around. The golden ringlet that she'd threatened me with exploded from her hand. It was met with an impressive flare of magic that swelled around it and devoured it. Flushed and angry, Peter took the opportunity to try and escape Dominic's hold. Dominic released him as Ileana recited the spell. The confidence that Ophelia and Peter wielded disappeared in a panicked reaction, their lips moving fervently, reciting spell after spell, trying to break the object and stop the spell. Fury washed over their faces as their magic weakened. Ophelia was the first to give up, backing away and returning to Celeste's cell. A last-ditch effort to cause harm. Pepper spray in hand, I looked for an opening to get to her.

Areleus got to her first. With weakened magic, the gold ringlets were no longer at her disposal. A finger flicked and released a pitiful puff of magic that seemed almost comical. Blistering rage roiled off her and she misdirected it to me, as if I'd discovered the Diax. I'd only made sure it was in their presence to do its job. She lunged at me, and I spritzed her face with the irritant. Relieved of his magic, Peter was faced with the same problem. The inability to fight the royals without magic. He tried. Turning to Dominic, he punched him. Dominic caught his hand mid-strike, grabbed him by his throat, and pinned him to the wall. I didn't miss the way he extended his fingers; with his diminished magic, calling for his claws was no longer an option. But his strength remained.

"Let me go," Peter squeaked, scratching at Dominic's hand. He fought until he lost consciousness. Through the chaos, Ileana let go of the concern she had for her son and returned her attention to the Diax that held the magic.

With the Book of Umbra in hand, she appeared frozen, seemingly unable to destroy the magic that held Dominic's and the Casters'. She'd lost her ruthlessness and cold-hearted objectivity.

"You don't have your claws," she said to Dominic. He would adapt, but razor-sharp weapons at easy disposal was something he'd not quickly adapt to. How could he?

"Do it," Dominic commanded.

That moment of hesitation cost them because Areleus snatched up the Diax and gathered up tidal waves of magic.

Securing the Diax in the palm of his hand, he demanded that Ileana give him the book.

"He doesn't have his claws. I do. I will not hesitate to take your heart," he said at her refusal. The cool indifference in his words was echoed in his eyes. Immortals were difficult to kill. Dominic hadn't been too enthusiastic about telling me the ways in which they could be killed.

Drawing back her lips in a challenging sneer, her fingers made distinct movements and the air thickened with an energy that reminded me of how it felt when she removed the magic in the warehouse. But she didn't have time to create the sigils to create the magic.

Magic gathered into a black cloud. Orange coiled around the cloud, making it bob erratically for release. Areleus was not impressed. Releasing force like a cannon, Areleus's hand countered and sent her magic back at her. A quick rotation and sidestep took her out of its pathway. Instead, it hit the wall, making an explosive cloud of drywall and wood.

Ileana's eyes narrowed on him. She shook her head and a look of disappointment swept over her face. "You're not going to honor your word?" she said in a tepid voice.

"We agreed he's not the same and that his human may be his fall."

"Or his redemption. One I thought I saw in you last night. I gave you the Book of Umbra in good faith. My hope was that you wouldn't use it against us—against your son to obtain greater power." *Well that was a damn lie.* She delivered it with such sincerity and authenticity, I doubted I'd ever trust anything she said again. She shook her head. "I thought we also agreed about the dangers. In the wrong hands, it's a danger to us all. Dominic sacrificed his magic. I thought we'd agreed we'd sacrifice the book. Allow it to be destroyed with the Diax."

Although she seemed to be taking his tight-lipped quiet as contemplation, I saw it as indomitable defiance. Her voice softened to an entreat. "You are well positioned, and even in his weakened state, do you doubt Dominic's ability to be a force and a needed ally? If you do this, your future will be at risk. Don't do this," she warned.

Making the choice for him, she continued with the spell without waiting for an answer.

A simple swipe of his hand across the air, and the Book of Umbra was in his hands. "We agreed," he asserted again.

With a sharp look that warned against stopping him, his mouth moved fervently. Ileana's lips drew back in a sneer of challenge, and her fingers made sharp rote movements. The Diax and Book of Umbra were ripped from his grip. He tossed a spell and moved in equal measure to snatch the objects back. The battle of magic left the objects hovering in the air.

"Father, don't," Dominic said. The room quieted. Areleus's eyes widened for just a second at the reverence in Dominic's voice. "Nothing good will come from this. I'm warning you."

But Areleus's cold, avaricious eyes couldn't be reached. In an act of desperation of a person who no longer had magic, Ophelia made an unsuccessful lunge at the Book of Umbra and the Diax. She was stopped by Anand, who dragged her and Peter back and placed them in a cell. Even if she'd managed to get the objects, without her magic, it would've been in vain.

"Warn." Areleus scoffed. "You've put yourself in a position that your warnings mean nothing. Soon you won't have any power or influence. Are you stronger than a witch now? Can you defend yourself against a shifter?"

He sneered, the shock from the display of familial feeling gone. "Will you be a match against vampires?"

Dominic moved with preternatural speed, slamming his father against the wall, his forearm pressed against Areleus's throat. Dominic suffered the pain of Areleus using one claw while he held on to the Diax.

Icy blue waves tugged between them, their eyes locked. I tried to determine who was producing the magic or if it was a combination of them both. When it vanished, Areleus's hand trembled as he attempted to release the Diax without success. His eyes dropped to the symbols that crawled up his arms, similar to those that had marked Helena when her magic was restricted.

When the Diax fell from his hands, anger washed over his face. Realization soon followed when both the Diax and the Book of Umbra began to crumble into dust.

Lowering Areleus to the ground, Dominic glanced down at the wound he'd acquired that was undoubtedly healed. He grabbed his father's fisted hand before it could connect with his face. The ease with which he did it left Areleus dejected. He no longer had the speed and strength that came with magic.

"I warned you. When has Mother ever fallen for your charms? You didn't persuade her to allow you to see the Book of Umbra. She gave you the opportunity to be your own undoing. *You* were the sacrifice of magic." He stood and stepped back, extending his fingers to reveal his claws again with a smirk.

"You asshole," Areleus spat out, his fingers lashing out to summon magic that he no longer possessed. It would take him time to get used to that.

"Exactly. When I need to be, I'm worse than you are. I didn't concede out of weakness or veneration for you. It was only a matter of time before the opportunity arose where your thirst for power and hubris would blind you to the flaws in your actions that would destroy you."

With a whirl of his finger, one of the cell doors opened. Dominic grabbed Areleus's arm and twisted it behind his back, depositing him in the cell.

Turning from his father's yells, curses, and promises of violence, he nodded at his mother before taking my hand.

His eyes traveled over every exposed inch of me, looking for injuries.

"I'm fine." More than fine because it was over. Really over. Breathing a sigh of relief, I averted my eyes from the bodies that remained.

Following my gaze, he held me tighter. "I'm sorry you had to see that."

Seeing it wasn't as bad as being there when it happened. I wanted to go into the cell and knee Peter in the crotch again. Positioning himself to obscure the sight of the fallen guards, Dominic guided me to another exit and led me back to his room where he told me he'd return soon. I doubted it would be soon; he had a great number of things to take care of.

Including his father.

17

As I'd predicted, Dominic didn't return soon. I'd showered and fallen asleep and was awoken by the earthy aroma of cedarwood and the hints of bergamot that lingered from his bodywash as his damp chest pressed against the back of the shirt I'd borrowed from his closet. Turning to face him, my fingers traced over his sharp jawline. I kissed him and when I pulled away, he pulled me closer, wrapping his arms around me as he deepened the kiss. He moved away with a sigh and a sharp, scrutinizing look. His hand found its way under my shirt, delivering soft tranquil strokes over my back and the curve of my ass. Dominic's eyes were a contrast to his touch.

"I don't know if you are incredibly brave or naively optimistic," he said gently.

"I'm a healthy dose of both," I teased. My response rounded off the edges in his keen eyes, but the look of consideration remained.

"I didn't think your father would betray you," I admitted. I did but wanted to believe he wouldn't. After Dominic conceding to never challenge him and seeing Dominic sacrifice some of his magic to save Helena and rid the world of the Dark Casters' magic, I thought Areleus would be satisfied. Not opt to betray his son and try to steal his magic and that of the Casters. It was a response to what I believed he had to be thinking. How could he not?

"The shades. What are your plans for them? Can't they be…I don't know, rehabbed or something? Anand can control them—"

"Within limitations and only when he is in their presence. If they escape again…" He sighed. "You may not agree with my mother's tactics most of the time, but sometimes being uncompromisingly pitiless is the answer."

I was constantly hit with the reality that things were darker and more violent in this world, and it reminded me again of how much I wanted to escape it.

"Helena."

His eyes followed mine to the door, where she stood, seemingly reluctant to enter the bedroom. Subdued humility was a poor fit for her. Her mouth opened and closed without a word spoken. Suspecting it was my presence, I started to move away to leave. She shook her head.

"Stay," she encouraged. "Siding with the Dark Casters for power was an inappropriate thing to do," she said softly.

What type of apology was that? My bad, betraying you just wasn't proper.

Securing a towel around him, Dominic rolled from the bed and pulled out a pair of jogging pants and slipped them on. He moved to stand in front of her, a tick in his jaw. "That is not an apology, Helena."

Her humility short lived, her chin tilted in rebellion. "I'm sorry that you displayed a weakness that made me feel an alliance with the Dark Caster would ensure true power," she hissed through clenched teeth.

Before Dominic could respond, I snapped. "That isn't one, either. How about I'm sorry I betrayed you when you were willing to sacrifice so much for my safety? Or, I'm a shitty sister and you deserve better? Maybe, I'm the worst, can you ever forgive me? Any of those are acceptable."

I grinned at Dominic's failing effort to suppress his laughter. After being with this family, I wanted to give my own family the biggest hug and bask in their special type of weird and unshakeable bond forged on unconditional love, grateful that it wasn't tainted by betrayal, attempted murder, and extreme measures to obtain domination.

Ignoring any of my suggestions, she shelved the self-indulgent look for a moment, although uncertainty peeked through. "What will happen to Father?"

"He will be banished. Without magic, he can't negotiate the various realms."

"They'll kill him."

At Dominic's cool indifference, she took his hand. "Will you not return his magic?"

"I can't even if I wanted to. It was destroyed. I suspect he'll spend the rest of his existence looking for a way to do so."

Helena displayed a stoicism that I hadn't managed. When he looked at me, I attempted to usher one. I couldn't. Agreeing with Helena made it more difficult.

"I will not leave him unprotected, a courtesy I wouldn't have received from him." He directed the answer to Helena, but his eyes searched my face. He returned the small smile I gave him.

Helena gathered his hands in hers and bowed her head. "I'm sorry." It was an unexpected earnest apology. My pessimism reared its head. I suspected the apology came from fear of ending up like her father rather than authentic redemption. Dominic never revealed his hand, which left him at an advantage. She had to assume that he had a way to deliver the same retaliation to her; after all, he'd discovered a means to restrict her magic.

"What will happen to me?"

Several moments ticked by, and worry creased Helena's brow.

"I don't know." His response left no room for further discussion and they looked at each other, expressionless. Helena nodded and left the room.

"Can you live here with Helena?" he whispered.

I didn't fear her, I just didn't like her. "I could live here with her, if I wanted to live here."

He turned to me and drew me close. "What are you saying?"

"I don't want this to be my world," I said. "We have to find another way for us to be together."

The air grew thick with tension. His features were blanketed with an emotion I couldn't place. His frustration and disappointment resonated within me, stirring a need to ease it.

Dominic's thumb roved lightly over my lips, replaced by his lips. Soft, sensuous, and inviting. His kisses became deeper, coaxing me into a desperate need that he knew only he could sate. I pulled him closer. The heat from him enveloping us. Whatever doubt existed seemed to dissolve in that moment.

He pulled away and I found myself studying his carved features, stern eyes that softened when he looked at me, and disposition that managed to depict his duality: a being who controlled the darkest and worst of the magical kind who must act without any humanity, and a person who desperately clung to some fragments of that humanity in order not to be possessed by power and cruelty.

I was seconds from asking if he could walk away from it and live a normal existence, but the fear of his wrath stilled my tongue.

"I don't want to lose you," he admitted, "but it's impossible for me to completely leave this."

"I don't expect you to. It won't be easy, but we'll make it work. Somehow."

He studied my face. "Little Luna," he whispered. His lips curled into a smirk. "Humans." He still had a hint of disdain for the magicless. "They will never know how hard you fought for their safety."

"Wasn't just theirs. I don't want to be subjugated."

"I would never let that happen."

"I know you wouldn't. But why subject the world to more fighting and you to more challenges of trying to keep me safe? I prefer not to be the exception. I want safety to be the rule. Living alongside supernaturals, ignorant of their existence, is the best option. My motives weren't that altruistic. You would have done whatever was necessary to achieve the same outcome."

"No, I wouldn't have," he responded curtly.

Do I respect the candor or be appalled by it? He leaned in and kissed the tip of my nose.

"I wish that I could. I wasn't lying when I said we lose some of our humanity to continue to live. I need you because you are an anchor that will keep me tethered to it. I love you because of who you are but also because you have that unique ability to do that for me."

I blinked back the tears, but a few managed to escape. He swept them away with his thumb.

"I love you, too. I want to be that person for you." I was confident we would make it work and that it would be difficult at times, but it didn't matter. I wanted it to work.

"Will you stay today?"

"Of course."

His soft lips feathered over mine before he sighed into a chaste kiss that quickly heightened into a devouring kiss. His tongue parted my lips and teased and taunted me with the promise of more. I welcomed the enveloping heat of his magic and the sensual caresses that accompanied it. With each second gaining a new appreciation for the mastery and the magnetism of it as it drew me to him.

Easing me to my back, his body melded over mine as he nestled between my legs. Then he pulled away, leaving me breathless and panting.

He flashed me a devilishly alluring look that sent shivers cascading over me, then pulled his shirt off me and tossed it aside.

Mischief glinted in his gaze as with effortless sinuous movement, his nails lightly grazed my skin along the same path as his tender kisses. He took my nipple into his mouth, teasing it with his tongue, the taunting grazes of his teeth coaxing a smile from me, then a moan. Continuing his tantalizing journey, he positioned himself between my legs, kissing my inner thighs before spreading them farther apart. His tongue flicked over my clit, sending shivers of pleasure through me as I fisted the sheets and moaned his name. The warmth of his breath when he chuckled sent a tremor through me. His tongue delved deeper, bringing me to an overwhelming climax. I couldn't help but cry out as waves of ecstasy and pleasure pulsed through my body, leaving me completely pliant.

Dominic removed his pants and slithered into his dominant position over me. His kisses were filled with a desperate need and primal lust that pushed me again into the depths of desire. As my fingers slid down his back, my nails lightly grazed over his skin. My hand continued its trail until I held his cock. As I stroked his hardness, his groans of pleasure caused his chest to reverberate against mine. Dominic pulled from the kiss and held my gaze as I guided him into me. The rhythmic thrusts of his hips started off slow, gradually building up to a frenetic pace. I wrapped my legs tightly around him, matching his intense movements, both of us seeking our pleasure.

An unexpected gasp escaped my lips when Dominic lifted

me, still kneeling, pushing himself even deeper inside me while he held me up. In response, I released a desperate moan of satisfaction into the passionate kiss we shared. The sensation of his dark magic danced over my skin, intensifying our connection. His movements were dark and feral, relentlessly chasing the climax that awaited us. I came first. The aftershock of my pleasure wracked my body. I pulsed and tightened against his hardness, coaxing him into an explosive release that elicited a low, primal growl.

His voice, laced with a rough edge of need and desire, alternated between whispering deliciously naughty details of what he longed to do to me and declaring his deep affection. It was an intoxicating combination that gave me a profound sense of contentment as I clung to him, reveling in the raw intensity of our union. Our bodies remained connected, locked in a fierce embrace. In that moment, our chaotic and complicated world faded away and it was just the two of us.

18

Dominic's request for today became three days. The day the Dark Casters and Areleus had been divested of their magic, we'd spent in his room together, enjoying the gentle ache of pleasure as Dominic found reprieve with me. We left the room only for food and the bed for showers. The second day, I didn't see him that much because he was dealing with the aftermath of that day. I spent time in the library, finding books that would hold my attention and devising a story to tell others that was believable enough but wouldn't reveal the existence of shifters, vampires, witches, and other magic wielders and would garner enough compassion from Cameron to allow me to return to work at the cafe. Four hours into the task and I had nothing. Telling her the truth would either have her seeking psychological help for me or in such complete awe of my mere survival that it would warrant my job back. I couldn't tell her the truth.

In the afternoon of the day I'd decided to leave, Dominic and I were walking through the garden with its peculiar black flowers. I gently touched the petals of the roses, feeling the weight of Dominic's eyes on me and the dark surroundings prophetic.

"Why don't you want to live here?" he finally asked.

"Because it's not where I belong. Without magic, I'm a human in the Underworld. I'd have to leave my friends and family. My life. I liked my life."

"You're free to leave. You wouldn't be imprisoned."

"I know, but I wouldn't be really free. I'd be reliant on you or the Trapsen to travel between the two worlds. And we run the risk of my possession of the Trapsen being discovered and someone taking it. You can't believe that others wouldn't desire something so valuable. Even if not for nefarious purposes, it would be wanted out of sheer curiosity. Areleus could try to take it and use it as a way to return. Or I could accidentally misplace it. It's not that I dislike it here, but me living here and trying to hold on to my life would be difficult."

At the mention of his father's name, he looked away from me. Forty-eight hours after the loss of his magic, Areleus had gone through the first stage of grief and was lingering in the stage of anger, demanding nearly hourly to speak to Dominic.

"If anyone can make this arrangement work, we can. Things are different for you, too. You could easily do like the others and live among the humans unnoticed." Or maybe not. His looks commanded attention. Despite his ability to mask his eyes, he possessed a distinct aura. He'd never go unnoticed, although no one would ever determine the reason why.

"When will Areleus leave?" I asked.

"Tomorrow. He has a house where he will live. I'll take that time to reestablish the rules with the Conventicle and make sure they are acting as one. I won't intervene with how they handle the Awakeners." A hint of sadness moved over his face so quickly, I would have missed it if I hadn't been fixed on the most minute changes in him. The barrier he erected to do his job objectively was sliding in and out of place to speak with me and deal with everything that was going on.

I turned, following Dominic who kept a careful eye on his sister as she approached. A sullen expression was on her face and her hands were balled into fists as if she needed that reminder not to bare her claws. Her energy hummed with restrained anger. I suspected she had just been informed by Ileana that she would be returning to the Vita with her.

"You're banishing me, too?!"

When Dominic didn't immediately answer, she made another demand. His cool silence pushed her into fits of anger and creative uses of "fucker" and other four-letter words that wouldn't curry any favor or encourage him to reconsider. Dominic displayed a cool amusement at her tantrum and display of rage that in the past were given a pass or coddled.

Now it was met with no reaction except Dominic's low modulated response. "Bye, Helena. I hope we do see each other. But for now, I don't want to see your face. You have your magic, and I promise not to take that from you *if* you honor my wishes for you to leave. In time, I hope my trust in you can be restored."

I understood her fledgling look of hopelessness and ire. In her place, I would have felt similar emotions because Dominic's interaction reeked of indifference. She wanted more—any display of emotion—because I figured she knew, like most, that the opposite of love isn't hate, it's indifference.

In an effort to control her anger, she took several slow measured breaths. With each one, her pinched expression eased. "I hope in time it can be restored, as well. If you tell me what I can do to make that happen, I'll do it." She pushed the words out through tightly pressed lips. I had to give her credit at the effort she made to sound sincere.

He nodded, accepting what appeared to be a tacit apology. "Leaving is a start." Slowly turning, she came face to face with Ileana, whose appearance surprised me although it was obvious Helena and Dominic were not surprised.

"We'll leave together," Ileana instructed in a tone that gave me the impression that despite her unwavering support and allegiance to her daughter, Helena would have to endure the consequences of her actions.

"May we talk?" Her gaze bobbed between the two of us, leaving me unsure.

"Meet me in my office."

At a loss, I glanced at Dominic who gave me a wayward grin. "She would like to speak to you and then me."

How did he get that from her statement?

Her approach seemed more like a stalk. A predator to prey. I rooted my feet in place because it was the only thing that would keep me there. Ileana's slow advance didn't lead to confidence. I stood taller at her intrusive gaze that bored into me.

She nodded. "You are lovely and kind. An unremarkable human," she said decisively.

"Uh, thank you?" *Is it really a compliment when the insult outweighs it?*

"It is not meant as an insult. You don't have the ability to remove empathy as a matter of recourse."

"I don't have the ability to be cruel," I surmised.

She nodded as if that was a flaw and I'd accepted it. I pushed down the desire to debate the issue because I would never change her mind.

"Now, do you crave power on any level?" She considered that statement. "I guess you're not quite human. Dominic tells me you never inquired about your magic being returned. He would have done what it took to do that and yet, it wasn't important to you."

"He's important to me, not the magic. I don't want that or

—" Catching what was going to be an insulting response, I modified my words. "I just want my old life back. I liked it."

"You realize he can't abandon who he is?"

"I know. I'd never ask him to. But we'll make it work. I know we can."

She looked around the garden and over the estate, her brows netting together. I knew she was aware of me declining to stay with Dominic in the Underworld.

Her assessing gaze left me feeling bare and vulnerable. Me gawking at her disarming smile was weird. It bloomed effortlessly over her face and radiated a warmth and genuineness that I'd never seen in her. Sharp eyes softened, and peeks of the compassion that moments ago she attributed to my flaws, glimmered in her eyes.

"Do not be his fall, okay?"

I nodded when the words didn't come. Although there was kindness in her words, I heard the undertone of threat.

But even without the subtle threat, that wasn't my intention.

19

We lay in bed, Dominic's adept fingers moving languidly over my body. I relaxed as he lay nestled between my legs, where he'd moved after we woke. We'd managed to get in a shower and brush our teeth before breakfast, although we never got to breakfast; we knew it was a bad idea to shower together. Spent from the shower sex, we sank back into the soft sheets. It was hard to separate and do something as mundane as eating when it might be a few days before we'd see each other again. He had to take care of the business waiting for him, and I needed to reassemble my shattered life.

Sinking my fingers through his hair, playing with the strands, I was trying to focus on his questions, which was getting increasingly difficult because my body craved to respond to his touch.

"What are your plans again?" He repeated the same question he'd asked before bed the night before.

"Get my job back." I beamed.

Warm breath from his chuckle brushed over my skin. "I see your plan to get your job back hasn't advanced any more than yesterday."

"I do have a plan. Puppy dog eyes and apologies. That's plan A," I said, giving him a light smack across his back when his chuckle transitioned to his tongue grazing over my belly. "I plan to tell her it was urgent family matters and hope she doesn't ask further questions."

He repositioned himself until he straddled me. With an arm on each side of me, he held my eyes. The banked fire in them drew me in until they extinguished into deep amber. He seemed to understand I didn't want to discuss my job any further. I really didn't have a plan but desperately wanted to return.

Dominic studied me for several moments. The weight and intensity of his scrutiny made me drop my eyes from him several times. It felt like he was stripping away the layers of a facade I had haphazardly erected. Despite the affection that peeked through, it felt invasive.

"Why didn't you even inquire about a way for your magic to be returned?"

"It was never mine," I said. "If I had it, I'd be tethered to the magical world. If it's ever discovered that magic could be taken and harnessed for someone's own purposes, I'd be a target. Or, fear of the type of magic I possessed would open me up to attempts to stop it by killing me. Even if it was determined I'd never be a risk to anyone, the magic would always be coveted. I don't want a life constantly upended by requests for alliances. Being with you will come with some risks, I know that. I don't want magic to add to that."

"Risks?" He chuckled.

"My life being endangered because of you is funny?"

"Not at all. Of all the things to worry about, that should not be a concern. I give you my word no one will come near you, for any reason. Your life will be more protected than theirs because their existence hinges on it." His chest reverberated with the growl in his words.

Pressing a gentle kiss to his lips, he deepened it. His lips rested on mine.

"Say it."

I smiled against his mouth. "I love you."

"I love you, too."

20

I had given it two weeks to make sure everything had settled and that I wouldn't be met with any more surprises. Except for the updates Dominic gave me during his visits, my life had returned to normal—somewhat normal. The machinations that existed in the shadows would never allow me to live a completely normal life. It was impossible to believe that.

When I entered the café of Books and Brew, Emoni waved and gave me an excited grin and overly enthusiastic thumbs-up, which did not have the effect she intended. If she felt the need to be so animated and optimistic, it was to help alleviate some of the hopelessness of the situation. My hands shaking was an unexpected response to entering Books and Brew. When I sent Cameron a text asking to speak with her, receiving her quick response made me hopeful, but the closer I got to actually chatting with her, the scarier it seemed.

Come on, Luna, you've been around shifters, dark lethal magic, vampires, deity-like beings, and witches. Nothing should shake you.

The pep talk didn't work. I'd been tossed into those situations operating on adrenaline and the desperate need to survive. Despite death being the possible outcome of those interactions, this one seemed scarier. It was ridiculous. But I felt the way I felt.

I liked my job and working with my best friend made it better. The owner was kind, but it was a big ask to allow me to return to work after having been gone for so long. I hadn't even given her the consideration of calling out. Or the courtesy of an outlandish excuse. I was nervous, hoping that a personal emergency as an excuse would suffice.

My eyes met Cameron's and the ebullient smile she flashed quickly faded as if she was reminded that she needed to be angry with me. There was a subtle sheen of worry in her look when she beckoned me to follow her into her office. Small, and often used as secondary storage, the office wasn't tidy. It never was. Used so infrequently, the computer was surrounded by discarded papers. A few post-its were lined in a row on the table. The smell of coffee and vanilla wafted in the air.

There were boxes of books and supplies stacked in the corner. The long black adjustable standing table that she used, always in the standing position. A chair that looked too comfortable not to take advantage of. A wooden chair positioned in front of it for conferences. It didn't invite comfort, so conversations while sitting in it were short and sweet.

Cameron didn't direct me to the chair but directed me to the sofa crammed into the opposite side of the room. It was comfortable in the way a well-used sofa is. Firm but cozy and offering a warmth that relaxed those seated. She handed me a water from the mini fridge and sat at the opposite end of it, turning to me.

Her brow inched up, she took a drink from her own bottle, and pushed out a sigh in a heavy exhalation. "Where have you been?"

The concern etched in her features made me want to spill it all, no matter how unbelievable and strange.

"Reginald told me that you were in deep." The tarot reader who claimed to be a witch was the first person I called after the incident with the book that started it all, teaching me to stay far away from unique untitled books. It was then I knew his claims to magic weren't true. He did his best to help me, but the other *witches* he knew were just as fictitious as he was. And he couldn't keep a secret, but since most people didn't believe in the occult, it was safe.

"He went on to insinuate that magic was involved." The way she waved off that detail, I assumed she thought he was being ridiculous to keep from providing the truth. "Emoni was quite guarded and evasive whenever I inquired about you. She seemed as worried as I was, which made me believe she didn't know, either."

My head lowered, I fidgeted with my cuticles and nails, knowing that if the hurt and worry in her words showed just a fraction on her face, the dam would break and I'd be retelling the story to a nice doctor who could give me the help she thought I needed.

When I finally lifted my gaze to meet hers, I'd shored up the ability to not crumble.

"I wish I could tell you everything, but I can't. This doesn't give you a reason to consider letting me come back, but the situation was unavoidable. You're the last person I'd knowingly disappoint, and I hope you know that." What I'd practiced was better, and I hadn't anticipated my voice breaking and the amount of emotion it held. I loved my job. This was one of the few jobs where the owner said we were a family, and it was true.

The longer she took to respond, eyes narrowed with uncertainty, searching my face for more, I knew the further she was from approving my return.

"Okay," she said finally. "But it's a trial for now. I'll put you on the schedule, but if this happens again, I won't entertain speaking with you again."

She stood and I followed. A half smile curled her lips. "Now Emoni can get back to normal. She's surprisingly mellow when she's worried. The customers were concerned."

I was sticking with the belief in pretty privilege. Her snark was amusing and cute because it came from a person who made extra money from her looks.

"I'm happy to be back." Rocking back and forth, the hug-urge was strong. Cameron was the first to initiate it. I welcomed her typical genuinely warm embrace.

One less issue weighed on me as I put the pieces of my life back together bit by bit.

***

Next on my list was to have the needed conversation with Forest to update him. In the two weeks since my return, he'd visited once and never discussed what I'd revealed to him, although I could tell he was still curious. Anytime he seemed like he was gearing up to ask questions, I redirected him. I'd become exceptionally skilled at it because of my conversations with Emoni. She had a dangerous combination of fascination and revulsion with the supernatural world, which made forgetting about it, or even losing interest in it, impossible. She watched people differently, blazing curiosity and inquisition toward everyone she encountered. That was her trying to determine if they were human or a clandestine supernatural. I had to constantly remind her that staring and unyielding scrutiny bordered on creepy. Over the past few days, it had diminished, but she remained hyperaware of everyone and the possibility of them not being human.

During my last visit with Forest, he insisted, "The next time we meet, we're going to discuss everything you've been avoiding telling me. I want to know it all." There was no room for debate or refusal. And I didn't want that out. He deserved to have answers.

It was his idea to meet at the creamery. I guessed navigating the truth about supernaturals was easier while scarfing down his favorite flavor: mint chocolate. Waiting for me in front of the ice-cream shop, he was attentively scraping the last bit of ice cream from a small cup.

He accompanied me into the shop. I left with a small waffle cone. He had a large bowl of mint chocolate.

"I'm not sharing," he announced, giving my single scoop cone a derisory look.

"We'll see," I teased, following him outside. We decided to walk instead of sitting at one of the tables where our conversation could be overheard.

The farther we walked, the deeper we fell into seemingly benign conversations that made Forest fidgety while he geared up for our actual conversation. A spirited curiosity played over all the angles of his face, and there was a strain in his voice as he struggled to tamp it down and not rush his questioning.

"Thank you for not freaking out when you couldn't reach me. You deserved better, and I'm sorry," I said, giving him a segue. I'd returned home to several missed messages and texts from him.

"I didn't have a lot of choice. When we spoke, you seemed so confident and capable of navigating things. So, I tried not to worry."

"I did?"

He nodded. "Yeah, you did. And you had Emoni and her knife skills." He laughed. I joined him in it. It died down with his heavy sigh. "What happened?"

I couldn't help but be impressed by his unwavering composure as I provided him an unabridged version of everything that had occurred.

"Areleus was going to kill his wife!" he blurted, his steps

coming to an abrupt halt. His eyes pivoted to me. Some of the color had drained from his cheeks, and his lips were parted in shock.

I corrected him with, "They aren't married."

"That's better!"

"No. Their world is different. Darker. Complex. It's shocking, but in the context of their world, not terribly unexpected."

"Seems like a reason for you to stay away from Dominic," he offered in a concern-laden tone.

When I didn't respond, he moved in front of me. Forest's expectant look pleaded for an answer. My silence withered his expression into worry. "Luna?"

"I want to, but I love him. I don't have magic and I have no relevance in their world."

"Can you be irrelevant when you're dealing with Dominic and his new position? Whether or not you accept it, you will indirectly be a part of that world if you're with him."

"I'm not part of that world, just his."

The worry creases relaxed and he huffed out an exasperated breath. "That's semantics, Luna. But if you make me worry about you again, I will have to make you end that relationship."

His jaw ticked while he sealed his lips into a tight line to suppress his laughter.

"Even you don't believe you have that ability."

He shrugged. "It was worth a try."

I was pleased when our conversation wandered from discussions of other worlds to another of his endeavors.

"You know, I've considered writing. Recently your life has been so fantastical and interesting, it would be fun to—"

"Don't," I rushed out in a tone harsher than intended. It was different than the *Discovery of Magic* Reginald had given me, which was steeped in misinformation. Forest knew intricacies of the world that demonstrated insider knowledge, and if it was ever discovered that he was my brother, it would put him at risk. "I don't want to give anyone any reason to be concerned about you and your knowledge of them."

"And that precisely is the concern."

I cringed at the people who'd invaded our space. Their imperceptible movement gave the illusion that they glided with the wind. Vampires. And we were surrounded by them.

They were unfamiliar to me, but it was likely that I'd seen them before. The faces of the supernaturals who attacked me were etched into my mind. I'd never forget their faces. The two male vampires were dressed casually, one in a textured pale green polo shirt and jeans, the other in a relaxed white button down and chinos. The third, a woman, wore navy ankle pants and a peach-color Henley tucked in. Each wore a pleasant warm smile that would lead casual observers to believe we were friends engaged in conversation. However, there weren't any casual observers, just me, Forest, and the vampires. Moments ago, there had been a stream of traffic and a few pedestrians. I wondered which witch I had to thank for the privacy.

The woman's smile widened to expose her fangs, prompting a sharp intake of breath from Forest. Her cool, calculating eyes jerked in my direction before she sneered at my lack of reaction.

I wasn't fearful. Instead, I felt increasingly annoyed. That response didn't go unnoticed by the other vampire. His gaze lingered on me for a long moment, his lips dipping into a rueful frown.

"We'd like to invite you to come with us. We have questions that need answers and concerns that need to be addressed," the frowning vampire said.

My eyes trailed over each one of them before I blew out a breath. "This feels more like a demand than an invitation."

"You're free to decline," the vampire in the jeans offered.

Predatory cold eyes swung in Forest's direction. "But he can't. We need to discuss the information he has about us and how negligent he's been in guarding that information."

Color drained from Forest's face when I glared at him.

Forest, what did you do?

As if he'd heard me, he tore his gaze from me and lowered his head.

There was no way I'd let Forest leave with them alone. From their restrained predatory looks, I knew they were waiting for us to bolt so they could engage in a chase.

Filled with disappointment, I acknowledged to myself that I was once again being pulled into their world and that Dominic's assurance had been wrong. That was the hardest part to accept. Was Ophelia right? Had I weakened him or ruined his standing among the supernaturals to the point they didn't feel the need to abide by his requests?

I parted my lips to agree, which they seemed to take as a tacit agreement, and before I could actually commit, Forest and I were swept away. The mode of transport didn't bother me, but being in an unfamiliar room did.

Forest grabbed my arm, trying to steady himself from the disorientation and the unsettling feeling from vampire travel. Looking around, I knew this wasn't the Conventicle's new headquarters; it wasn't pretentious and luxe enough. The room was a simplistic modest office. A long oak desk was placed in the middle of the room where five people sat in inexpensive-looking task chairs. Their stern cold eyes fixed on us.

Bookcases flanked two tall cabinets. Sunlight struggled to stream through the small windows framed by raised blinds. In the opposite corner was a chevron-patterned lounge chair with a small side table next to it and an arched floor lamp. The set-up was incongruous with the rest of the room. Pristine white painted walls contrasted with the forest-green carpet that was in desperate need of replacement. I couldn't determine if this was their actual headquarters or a borrowed space.

Out of my periphery, I spotted two wolves to our right, positioned to attack, which ushered in fear I hadn't had before.

"Those are werewolves," Forest whispered in a low, tremulous voice. The wolves monopolized his attention, causing him to ignore the other threats.

One of the vampires who snatched us made a show of running his tongue over his teeth. Two of the five people I remembered as being aligned with the New Conventicle. I had no idea what camp the vampires were from. Dominic told me that defected Awakeners had been captured and dealt with. He didn't elaborate, and I chose to believe they had a speedy trial and had been sentenced to detainment by the Conventicle.

"You all are a pain in the ass. What do you want?"

It wasn't bravado, it was true anger. Some of it was directed at myself. I'd advocated for their safety and had been truly naïve about their potential to harm me. Dominic and Anand had captured the shades, who were no longer a risk to the supernaturals. *Had that act emboldened these assholes?* Now they were working without any fear.

A man, I suspected a witch, sauntered toward me. Shifters had an assured, predatory gait that made a person feel like prey even if they weren't. Vampires had a mesmeric fluid movement. Witches and Seers were the most human in their presentation, although witches possessed a distinguishable arrogance.

"You have the confidence of someone who still has Dark Caster magic. We were assured you didn't and that you were not a concern. But I am very concerned," he asserted with the certainty of someone who had proof. No one had proof, just speculation. I had no idea if Peter or Ophelia had ever confirmed that I could wield Dark Caster magic.

"Well you're wrong. I don't have magic. What I have is a headache from dealing with you all. Leave me and my brother alone. You don't bother me, and I won't bother you. Deal?"

He scoffed. "When his video was cleared, his memories should have been altered, as well. Your brother has been quite busy posting his tales on free story sites." It took an extreme amount of self-control to keep my eyes on the witch and not risk a glare at my brother. When he'd suggested writing about them, he conveniently left out he'd already uploaded stories. He'd always been a proponent of the ideology that it was better to ask for forgiveness than ask for permission. This time that propensity could cost him dearly.

"Do you know how many books there are about supernaturals, your politics and vulnerabilities?"

"Often they ring of ignorance and fantastical embellishments." With a wave of his fingers, the witch manifested a small stack of papers and handed them to me. I skimmed over them, afraid to devote too much attention to them and ignore my environment. Tamping down my anger, I vowed that Forest and I would discuss this later. Damage control was my priority. He'd written so much from the limited information I'd previously given him. What would he have done with all the new and specific information I'd just given him?

Turning to my brother, I whispered in his ear, trying to speak as low as possible to prevent being overheard. "They'll want to compel you to forget."

"I don't want that done. They're not fucking with my head," he said, his anger making it difficult to keep his voice to a whisper.

"Would you agree to a binding oath?" We weren't leaving here without the assurance of his confidentiality.

"Depends on what it is."

"There will be no oaths," the vampire interjected before we could discuss it further.

I whipped around. "It should be part of the discussion."

The witch's venomous laughter filled the room as he turned to the vampire. "An oath is acceptable. A *mortalitas* oath would suffice."

I assumed *mortalitas* was Latin. It wasn't a good sign that it was a derivative of *mortal*.

"It is a binding oath that will cause death if he breaks it."

Despite his sharp, angular features and pronounced chin, a rosy flush grazed the witch's cheeks, and his kind hazel eyes held hints of discernment but not cruelty. His relaxed t-shirt and ripped distressed jeans reminded me of Peter, especially the way he bared his teeth with his harsh smile.

"No. That's not remotely an option."

"Because your brother is as much of a liability as you. What type of oath did you expect? A slap on the wrist? A good scolding and reminder for him not to do it again? With the *mortalitas* oath, if he breaks it, we just need to clean up the mess once and never have to deal with that problem, or him, again."

"He will agree to an oath with reasonable terms," I countered.

"You really aren't in a position to negotiate. You're an unsettling aberration whose existence shouldn't be taken lightly. If others choose to regard your involvement with all the events that have occurred as coincidence, so be it. I won't."

With his rote movements and rapidly moving lips, a mist formed between his hands. When he stepped toward me, Forest and I took several steps back to keep the distance between us. I was about to tell Forest to run, when the door was flung open by a powerful burst of energy. The witch was suddenly airborne and slammed into the wall across the room. He crumpled to the floor in a heap.

"How dare you! There is an agreement." Madeline's voice boomed. The lights flickered at her anger.

"Agreement?" The witch sneered. "Does it mean anything if we remain at risk?"

"How are we at risk? The shades are gone, there aren't any more Dark Casters. And the Awakeners who challenged us have been imprisoned, where you all will soon join them."

"Wasn't that claim made before? Dominic and his family boasted of making it safe, yet many died because it wasn't true. We've almost been exposed countless times. Yes, the Awakeners are imprisoned, but how many survived their capture to be given the courtesy of imprisonment rather than death?"

She jutted out her chin and pierced him with a hard look. "We have more autonomy and control than we have ever had, a unified front, and an alliance with the royals that benefits us. And his only request was to leave her alone. You fucking idiots!"

Magic exploded from her, sending everyone slamming into the walls. Except for the werewolves. Impervious to her magic, one wolf lunged at her. With a swift swipe of her hand, the vacant chairs careened into the wolf. One of the bookcases hurled into the other wolf.

Madeline's hands moved in sharp, distinct strikes. Eyes blazing with rage and fury, her frown ensured that they'd regret breaching the agreement. As Dominic had said, she appeared to be protecting me as if it were her own life. Seemed to be retaliating like the threat was to her. Fear crept onto their faces but quickly bloomed into satisfied smiles. The female vampire had Madeline pinned against her chest, her neck wrenched to the side to expose the vulnerable vessels in it.

"Shall we discover whether my fangs are faster than your magic?" she said against Madeline's neck. A crushed look of defeat coursed over Madeline's face. Usually haughty and confident, she now wore a wary look of fatigue. She was the self-proclaimed head of the Conventicle, and I figured the past few weeks must have come with its own set of challenges. She probably had been battling on behalf of the supernaturals against Dominic, asserting and campaigning to keep her position with the addition of new members, and negotiating unity among them. It was enough to cause exhaustion. Dealing with the Awakeners had to have taken an emotional and structural toll. If they were dealt with too harshly, the Conventicle would be viewed as tyrants; too leniently, the rules would be more likely to be broken.

The room silenced and all eyes turned to Madeline and the vampire. Tension and indecision lay heavy in the room.

"If you hurt her, we will incur Dominic's wrath. Much of his concession came with that one request. Leave her and her loved ones alone. It hasn't even been a month and already it's been violated." Madeline sighed with disappointment.

"We give him too much unchecked authority. One person." The vampire holding Madeline scoffed. "We have every right to do our own investigation and not take—"

Her words suddenly cut off, she dropped to the floor, her head twisted into an odd angle before Dominic plunged a stake into her heart. He whispered several words and with a wave of his hands, she disappeared. He didn't even give her a true death where the body withers and turns to dust. Before they could put up any form of a fight, the other vampires received similar treatment.

I wasn't sure how I missed whatever he'd done to the others in the room. But they were now secured against the wall by a luminous band around their necks, fearfully watching the demise of the vampires.

Mouth open in horror, Forest took measured steps backward to the door. I ran to him.

"Don't run away."

"What the fuck, Luna?" His eyes widened and he froze

mid-step, shocked to the point he didn't breathe. Following his stare, I saw Dominic engaged in a fight with the werewolves. One that lunged at him was met with powerful kicks that pushed him several feet away. Before he could rebound to stand, Dominic's claws were piercing his chest and then throat, which ceased all movement. My eyes trailed Forest to the other werewolf, who looked as if he'd received a similar ending, achieved in the short time it had taken me to look at the people pinned against the wall.

I returned my attention to Forest for a moment before looking at Anand and the cadre of guards from the Underworld who waited near the door. Catching Anand's attention, I made a poor attempt to nonverbal communication. Anand's brows drew together.

"No one's going to help?"

"Does he look like he needs it?"

Forest looked lost. Unable to move forward or back, he was floundering for an exit strategy.

I took his hand in mine. "It's fine. Just look at me," I coached him in a low, calming voice. There was no sense of pride in my ability to remain calm to the macabre soundtrack of unfettered violence.

He attempted for a second but whether it was morbid curiosity or revulsion he couldn't tear his eyes away. "Dominic?"

I nodded, following his gaze to Dominic who was standing in front of the supernaturals fastened to the wall. Madeline had put a significant distance between her and an enraged Dominic.

"I attempted to stop it," she said.

"I know. My anger will not be misdirected to you. You may leave if you wish, or stay so you understand how serious I am about Luna's safety."

"As per our agreement, the Conventicle should—" Madeline said.

"No way in hell. I made one request. One fucking request." The lights pulsed with his anger and stifled the room. "To leave her alone."

"We just needed to know," the cruel witch from earlier gasped out in a weak voice.

Dominic moved toward him in measured steps, taking slow breaths, I assumed to calm himself. But the baleful look remained. Standing directly in front of the witch, Dominic flicked his finger, and the witch's head jerked up to look him directly in the eyes.

"Madeline, tell me what I said during the meeting to all there."

Relaxing her tightly pressed lips, she said, "The agreement was that you wouldn't intervene with that of our world unless requested. That you would continue to imprison Celeste until we can undo the curse, protecting her life so that we can live. And you agreed not to intervene without our formal request unless it violated the safety of humans or if Luna was put in danger." She looked at me. "If she, her friends, or family were ever endangered, it would be handled without discussion or mercy."

"It was agreed upon, correct?"

She closed her eyes and nodded. Counterarguments and protests withered into a sullen look.

"Your witches should be the most determined to adhere to this agreement. How easy it would be to wipe out the strongest of your line."

I suspected all the witches who lined the walls were from the same bloodline.

He moved closer to one witch. "You were there." Quickly moving to the next, he studied him. "You were there."

He continued until he came to the last person. "Your face isn't familiar to me. Were you not aware of this agreement?" She had little available movement and turned her eyes toward Madeline. I suspected she knew and was debating whether Madeline would abet her lie.

Madeline took a deep breath. "All the witches were made aware of the agreement. I took it upon myself to impress upon them the gravity of it. The shifters and vampires were made aware as well."

He nodded and turned to face me.

"Luna, will you leave?"

I wanted to. I should have run away like I was being chased by an axe-wielding monster, but I couldn't. My feet were rooted in place. Lips parted but the words stuck in my throat. Which words? A jumble of them bounced around in my head. *Don't*, but what were their intentions for me? *Be the better person.* He had and they'd still violated his one request. *Okay.* Although I knew it was in my best interest to move, I was unable to do so even with the threat of potential violence.

Forest made the choice for me, grabbing my arm and hauling me out of the room. Anand and the guards formed a wall, preventing my return.

We left without looking back. I wouldn't look back. It felt like I was leaving it all behind. The human wall Anand and the guards had formed. The violence. The death. The drama and politics. The agreements. And perhaps Dominic.

Did I want to leave him, too? For the first time, I wasn't completely sure.

21

Forest shoved his hand through his hair, apologies and strings of curse words pouring from him like flowing water.

"They would kill to remain concealed?"

Relaxed back on the sofa, I massaged my temples, warding off the headache in order to summon the discipline to keep the sarcasm and desire to scold him at bay.

"I thought I'd made that quite clear. But obviously you didn't believe me."

He stopped his trek through my apartment. "That vampire was going to bite the witch," he eked out in a strained voice.

"No, she was probably going to do more than that," I corrected.

"I'm sorry." That was his seventh or eighth apology. "I knew it was serious but not that serious."

Why did he have degrees of seriousness? A group of powerful magic wielders wanted to remain concealed, and another group wanted to be revealed so they could subjugate humans.

As if he'd read my thoughts, he said, "I didn't have all the information." He shot me a wayward grin that comforted me more than it should have. "So technically, it's kind of your fault."

"I will punch you."

"Eh, the violence is rubbing off on you, too," he teased.

Despite his light-hearted banter he was still worried and frightened. But I didn't press it. We fell into an easy conversation about everything other than what had happened just hours before. But eventually, we had to leave the oblivion and denial.

"We're safe, aren't we?"

"Yeah." It was the most confident I'd ever felt because Dominic had honored his agreement.

Forest seemed reluctant to leave my side. I wasn't sure if it was because he was afraid or afraid for me. But he did answer the knock at the door.

"Dominic," he said, extending his hand and giving Dominic's a brusque shake.

"Forest, we finally meet." He looked down at his hand that Forest hadn't released. Holding it, Forest studied Dominic and the peculiar bank of flame that stayed in his eyes, although light enough at times to go unnoticed. They had Forest's attention.

I waited, wondering if he'd try to pull some protective brother BS. Instead, he said, "Thank you for saving our lives."

"Always." His assurance relaxed Forest even more. Dominic pulled him closer, his tone serious. "You *must* honor the request to never reveal anything to anyone. Can you do that?"

That didn't have to be said. Forest had been terrified into silence. I would have preferred it to have happened another way. But that's how it was. Forest turned to look between me and Dominic. The concern he had earlier when discussing Dominic wasn't there, or he'd discovered how to mask it.

Once Forest had gone, Dominic stood at the door. His

sharp eyes held mine. An inquiring look asking a question that he seemed reluctant to express.

"It shouldn't have gotten to that point. I'm sorry."

"You came."

"I always will." His eyes cast down with his sigh. "I hope I've made it possible for you to feel safe. To get back to your world the way you want it." He lifted his eyes and they met mine. His held a decisive look of contrition that made me unsettled. "When it comes to you, it's hard to be pragmatic. But not being so may do more harm than good. I don't see how they won't collide occasionally with me in it."

My heart pounded and the room felt too small. Before he could get the words out, I was standing in front of him. I kissed him. Sinking my fingers in his hair, I deepened it, removing any doubts that either of us had. I loved him. I wanted to be with him.

In our first encounter, he'd cared so little for the safety of humans, but now he'd made them a priority. He'd made compromises on my behalf. He loved me and showed it in so many ways. It was hard to despise having been pulled into his world when it had given me the opportunity to meet him.

His lips remained against mine when our kiss ended. "Are we okay?" he asked.

"We are more than okay. I'd rather deal with obstacles with you than not have you in my life. I want you."

He kissed me softly. "It goes without saying that I want you. All of you."

$\mathcal{E}$moni and I waved at Cameron, the personal items that we'd accumulated over the years packed up in a large Books and Brew promotional logo bag. Cameron's lips downturned into a deep frown made the departure feel worse.

"I'll miss you both," she admitted. Before we could respond, she gathered Emoni into a quick hug, who ended it abruptly when she pulled away. The hug between me and Cameron lingered. When she tightened her hold on me, I sank deeper into the warmth and comfort of it.

"I'll miss you, too," I told her.

"Me too," Emoni tacked on. "But if you start to miss our absence too much, just drive the twenty-five miles to the new location and wave at us," she added dryly, shaking her head at the maudlin display. "You two are being far too dramatic."

Cameron scrunched her nose at Emoni, who had been the voice of reason and clinical objectivity since Books and Brew had expanded to a new location. I was given an assistant managing position and Emoni was the manager of the café. My promotion was unexpected since it had been just a few days shy of a year since I'd gone MIA and Cameron graciously had given me my job back.

When I returned to work, I set my focus on earning her trust and for her not to regret employing me again. I booked local authors for readings and signings, hosted book clubs, game nights, and events that brought more attention to the store. It was easier to handle by successfully extracting myself from the supernatural world—well, everything except Dominic.

Dominic's response to when Forest and I were abducted ensured that we were left alone. I wasn't invisible to members or the Conventicle or the supernaturals who knew of my existence. When our paths crossed, we ignored each other. Visits from members of the Conventicle were steady. I hadn't determined if they were making sure no one bothered me or if it was to gawk at the woman responsible for Dominic issuing the threat that if any harm came to me, no matter how small, it would be met with terminally severe consequences. I'd accused him of being over the top and extreme, but I'd welcomed a return to a simpler world.

There was a notable uptick of people who made an effort to not be on the same side if I was walking on the sidewalk. I suspected that they were part of the supernatural community, and I was fine with their commitment to keeping their distance.

It still surprised me that the Awakeners had abandoned their plans to make their presence known and the Conventicle and the New Conventicle managed to work together without a civil war. They were a functioning unit. Dominic only had to intervene twice for a shifter and a witch sentenced to the Perils.

· · ·

Emoni and I slipped out of Books and Brew after giving Cameron another quick hug.

Emoni lingered at my car, one that I now needed since for the past six months I'd been living with Dominic in the apartment he once shared with Helena. She had freely relinquished it to prevent running the risk of interacting or having to see me. Something she had no qualms expressing to me. Somehow, she'd contorted the situation so much that I was now the blame for Dominic's response to her betrayal.

Although her time in the Vita was posed as time for her to reevaluate her life, she grumbled that she'd been imprisoned—her own version of the Perils—which I was confident was an exaggeration. Contrary to what Ileana had led me to believe, she wasn't as accepting of Helena's betrayal against Dominic and had addressed it.

Helena remained a beautifully dressed, self-centered, unnecessary source of violence and chaos, but she reined it in enough to abide by the agreement made with the Conventicle.

I peeled my focus from Emoni to eye the driver of the luxury sedan driving past us.

"That's not him," Emoni said.

It was an unreasonable practice that I couldn't manage to stop. Every expensive car with an older man in it who looked even remotely like Areleus drew my attention. After settling in his home, he left within a month. Dominic hadn't heard from him in over seven months and didn't seem concerned, confident that his time was being spent looking for a way to return his magic. He'd never accept the fall from power.

"I know this is ridiculous, but I'm worried about him."

"You're worried about the handsome, absurdly rich man who's having an identity crisis because he doesn't have magic?" She scoffed, shaking her head. "I'm sure there are more people deserving of that."

"He was the most powerful supernatural in the world and

now he's a man whose magic was ripped from him. He no longer has immortality and must live as a human."

"A man who's probably wreaking havoc looking for a way to get his magic and status back," she acknowledged.

I nodded. "A waste of his time."

"In his position, wouldn't you?" she asked, quickly waving off her query because she knew the answer. I wouldn't. My magic had been stolen and I had no desire to seek a way to retrieve it. Being free from magic allowed me to escape that world and move on, all while keeping Dominic. It was an absolute victory in my eyes.

Emoni eased away from me. "I have to go to rehearsal and then I have plans later. Call me tomorrow."

Since our return we'd spent more time together. Emoni's discovery of the supernatural world instilled a wariness that caused her to check on me more often than she had in the past. We weren't scheduled to work for the next few days, so she'd definitely visit or call.

It was better, but she lived with the anticipation of another upheaval of our lives and worse discoveries. For a while, it was the root of her apprehension about my relationship with Dominic. She wasn't convinced that it would be possible to have just fragments of that world. Having Dominic in my life meant having the supernatural world and all its violence, political unrest, and issues as well. I didn't blame her—at times I worried about the same. It had been a year since Dominic strolled into Books and Brew and questioned me about the *Discovery of Magic* that I carried, and my life devolving into something new and unsettling.

Dominic and I had managed what seemed like the impossible. Creating our own world together.

Emoni's level of alertness had diminished in the last four months as a result of Anand teaching her how to protect herself and becoming an exceptional source of information for any questions she had about supernaturals and their world. Emoni found comfort in knowing even the most minute details, despite her claims of wanting to be blissfully ignorant.

"Plans with Anand?" I asked.

She nodded. "I wish he'd come to watch the rehearsal, but he and Gus don't get along."

"What? Your boyfriend and the man who has had a crush on you for years don't get along? Shocking!" I teased.

She disregarded my comment with a grimace and a roll of her eyes. I still couldn't figure out why it was something she chose to ignore. Perhaps acknowledging it would somehow compromise the band.

"Have fun axe throwing," I said, opening the door to the car.

"How do you know that's our plans?"

"Because it's your plans almost sixty percent of the time. You weirdos," I shot back. "Jazz club then axe throwing. Movie and axe throwing afterward. Cooking class followed by axe throwing. Sex and then axe throwing."

"We've never!"

I smirked. "What? The sex and axe throwing are wrong? Or the wrong order?"

"I'm done with this conversation," she countered with a grin before leaving.

Dominic met me at the door with a roguish smile and a hug. His lips pressed against mine in a passionate, lingering kiss that sent small shivers through me. Despite waking up to his alluring looks, I was still captivated by them, and his touches continued to be as intensely inviting.

"How was your last day?"

"Emotional and bittersweet, until Emoni called us

dramatic and pointed out how easy it would be to visit if we wanted to see each other."

He chuckled. "Did you expect anything else from her?"

"I'm convinced she was more concerned about leaving so she could get to rehearsal so she could see Anand."

Smirking, his brow lifted. "I'm sure you pointed that out."

As the self-appointed hypocrisy buster, I was quick to point out her concern with me dating Dominic but not holding the same concerns when she started seeing Anand. She'd waved it away as it not being the same.

"No, it doesn't even bother her. She's shameless," I complained. "And she told me I could refer to her as the *Shameless* Lady of Wrath and Fire." She'd proudly adopted the title.

"Of course she did," he said, his fingers lacing through mine.

Noticing a levity to his smile and demeanor, I pulled him closer and traced the curl of his smile. "What's this about?"

"Madeline broke the spell today."

"Who's happier, the witches or Helena?"

Helena had been allowed to return home but was restricted from the Perils. Dominic took preventative measures to keep her from using Celeste as a bargaining tool against him or the witches.

"Of course the witches because their bloodline is safe. Helena doesn't know. Celeste will remain in the Perils. I don't trust that they can keep her properly imprisoned, and I can't risk her escaping and performing the spell again or worse." His deep intense eyes held mine. "Because I still don't trust Helena," he admitted, responding to my question before I could ask. "I'll lift the restrictions and give her full access to the entire home and see what happens."

I hadn't determined if the hurt of her betrayal had decreased or if he was better at hiding the tinge of anguish in his voice when he discussed her. He never had it when discussing his father, as if his betrayal was expected. But Helena's cut deep and left a lasting wound.

Helena no longer had the luxury of impunity for her actions that she'd taken for granted for so long. She wore that lifestyle change in the rigid weary frown that had become a fixture on her face. Or perhaps it just reasserted itself when I was around.

"My mother is looking forward to our visit to the Vita this weekend," Dominic reminded me in an abrupt but welcomed change.

"Me too." I'd grown accustomed to her ways and would go as far as to say that I liked her and she liked me, not just tolerated. I was liked as much as she could like "an expendable human," which was high praise for her. She still viewed me as an enigma for declining to explore options to retrieve my magic. Even with Dominic informing her that the probability was nearly impossible, she didn't understand me not exploring it despite the slimmest of chances.

"My mother has you this weekend, I'm sure Emoni will have you later this week, and I have you today."

"You always have me," I quipped, lifting to my toes and pressing a quick kiss to his cheek.

With a devilish glint in his eyes, he grinned. Lacing his fingers through mine, he led me to the kitchen. Placed on the table was a cake. Moving closer to get a better look, I saw it was an exact replica of the book *The Discovery of Magic*.

"This was our beginning," Dominic said. And a reminder of everything we'd gone through to get to this point.

I took in the intricate details of the cake, from the font of the title, the coloring of the cover, and the cream-colored pages.

He leaned down, the warmth of his breath brushing against my lips. "You're a witch," he said with the same assertion he had on our first meeting, but now he was teasing me with it.

I grinned. "No. Dark Caster...former Dark Caster. I'm just as dangerous."

His eyes glinted with dark amusement. He leaned in, capturing my lips in a deep, lingering kiss. "Of course you are, Little Luna. You're the peculiar human who captured my heart."

www.ingramcontent.com/pod-product-compliance
Lightning Source LLC
Chambersburg PA
CBHW030757190726
48285CB00003B/896